THE
PERCH

B. BUTTS WILLIAMS

THE
PERCH

MILL CITY PRESS

Mill City Press
555 Winderley Pl, Suite 225
Maitland, FL 32751
407.339.4217
www.millcitypress.net

Paperback ISBN-13: 978-1-66289-313-1
Hard Cover ISBN-13: 978-1-66289-314-8
Dust Jacket ISBN-13: 978-1-66289-472-5
Ebook ISBN-13: 978-1-66289-315-5

For every boy or girl who ever heard the words,
"Stop writing. There is no place for you. Go find a career."

For my dad who told me, "Yes, you can do it! You can do
anything you really want to do!"

For my community of supporters who encouraged me to
tell this story.

Table of Contents

Prologue

Fall, 1949

W hen Kizzy was four years old, she saw a dog eating a woman. Miss Sally was the woman's name. She lived down the street from Kizzy's house, next door to the juke joint on Carter and Boas Streets where the ladies of the night lived and conducted their business.

No one believed Kizzy when she told them about what happened to Miss Sally. She repeated what she saw again and again. Only her brother Leon, who was twelve (the middle of three brothers), would listen. He always listened to her stories.

They were sitting on the living room floor, working on a puzzle their mother had placed on a small table to encourage them to work together and learn how to solve problems without fighting and arguing. "Leon," Kizzy began. "Leon, I saw Old Pal eat Miss Sally! Miss Sally was screaming and screaming, and old Pal just ripped her arm off, and then he ripped the other one." Kizzy touched her left arm, then her right arm.

Leon looked at Kizzy in amusement as he sat across from her, a puzzle piece in his hand. "Kizzy, no way you saw that. Are you making this up?"

"I did see him do it. Old Pal looked at me first, and then he ripped her arms off." Kizzy's eyes were wide. "Miss Sally started kicking and wiggling her legs, then her entire body started shaking." Kizzy tried to mimic what she saw, throwing herself on the ground, shaking.

Leon sat there smiling. He loved listening to his little sister's stories, mostly because they were always scary. He had no idea why people always died in Kizzy's stories, but they did.

"Then Old Pal put his mouth around Miss Sally's throat and took a big chunk out of her neck." She sat up and looked at Leon. "He spit the chunk out, then chewed on it a bit, spit more out, and then took another chunk! Poor Miss Sally she stopped screaming after the first bite and her head dropped to the side."

Leon couldn't imagine Miss Sally with no arms and legs and a chunk out of her neck. Miss Sally was the nicest lady in the neighborhood. She often would walk over to Caldwell's house with an armful of books and magazines for all the kids.

"I tried to see her face, but I couldn't," Kizzy continued. "I started crying because I felt so sad. Miss Sally was my friend and so was Old Pal. So, I didn't know what to do."

Kizzy shook her head. "Leon, you should have seen Old Pal's face. His mouth was covered in blood, red, red like Alice's lipstick. I couldn't see his eyes or nose because Miss Sally's arms covered them." Kizzy stood up and walked over toward the large picture window in the living room and stood there as if she were on stage performing.

"Where were you, Kizzy, when you saw Old Pal eat Miss Sally?" Leon asked.

"Upstairs, I was sitting on the windowsill. You know Old Pal is my friend. He looked up at me as he dragged Miss Sally behind Mr. Meeks' broken-down blue truck. But I could see him anyway. I waved at him. Old Pal would look up at me as he started chewing on Miss Sally." Kizzy wanted to continue but noticed Leon had fallen asleep.

She wanted to tell him she saw Mr. Meeks come out of the house with a shovel and a big black bag, and poor Old Pal walking away from the broken-down car and throwing up in the alley across the street next to Mr. Meeks' house. Kizzy wanted to help him but didn't know how, just like she wanted to help Miss Sally but did nothing.

Spring, 1952

Kizzy was seven years old when she witnessed her mother, Emily Harrison Caldwell, being murdered. The memories of her mother's bullet-ridden, bloodied body and her limp head resting on Kizzy's lap were overwhelming and something Kizzy would never forget. A small crowd witnessed the dying woman's motionless body next to the girl and the bloodied mess nestled on the yellow and black checkered skirt the little girl wore. Drips of dark fluid flowed down the child's legs onto her white socks and black and white oxford shoes. Kizzy was covered from the waist down with her mother's blood, as were the concrete steps in front of the Caldwell home.

Later, family members and other folks would tell Kizzy, "Shut up, forget what you saw," "God has a plan," "We don't want any trouble," and "Stop making up stories, you will get somebody killed." Kizzy blamed herself for what happened to her mother. No one ever asked or wanted to hear what the little girl saw that day.

It was a few weeks after her mother's death when the dreams began. Kizzy would have the dreams over and over again. Kizzy saw herself sitting at the head of a large oval table decorated with candles, flowers, crystal glasses, and trays of food. A large window covered one side of the room, looking out at a river. Sitting around the table were maybe a dozen people. In the dream, Kizzy was all grown-up. Standing right behind her at the table was an unknown person.

In the dream, Kizzy would turn to the figure and ask, "Who are you?" "I'm your Watcher, your protector," the voice would reply.

"Are you real or am I dreaming?" Kizzy asked.

"I'm part of your destiny," the Watcher would say.

"What does that mean? I don't understand," Kizzy pleaded.

"You will understand in time," the Watcher said.

Kizzy always woke up after that exchange. She tried to determine what was real and what was an illusion. She was told her imagination would cause her great disappointment and she struggled after her mother's death to understand the difference.

Often, as a little girl, she would hear the adults she trusted say, "Stop making things up, lying, and saying you see things. People will think you're crazy." Over and over again, Kizzy was warned by the adults in her family: there is a thin line between insanity and sanity.

The Watcher became the only one who truly understood her demons.

Kizzy's mother died on a Monday afternoon, in May 1952. Later that evening Kizzy was kidnapped and discovered by two college students, Clay Barksdale, Jr. and Mason Johnson, who were on a field trip just outside Hershey, Pennsylvania.

Clay and Mason would later describe the feeling they had while with Kizzy at the farmhouse rescue as willing prisoners captured inside of Kizzy's private world.

Both men's destinies would later be linked with Kizzy's life.

After Kizzy's return home and later reunited with her family, she tried many times to explain what had happened to her, but no one believed the child's version of the events, and the kidnapping went unsolved for more than thirty years.

Kizzy learned at a young age how to exist between blurred lines and cope with multiple realities. She would be haunted by family secrets, revenge, power, and evil spirits only to be emboldened and guided by her own courage, the spiritual forces of her ancestors, and a thirst of her own for revenge and an undeniable will to pursue an uncharted destiny at any cost to herself or others.

Chapter 1

Genevieve's Curse

Lewis Family Plantation, Louisiana, 1856

Genevieve's eyes stayed fixed on them. She saw them enter from the small crack in the wall. She tried to reach for the large potato sack next to the bed near the wall. She thought if only she could crawl inside the sack, maybe, just maybe, they would not find her this time. She sighed and thought *no use, they always find me.*

Genevieve lay there waiting in the large dark room. She thought the sound of the men coming was like waiting to be taken to your own grave. Her stomach began to churn, and she felt sick. She heard them thumping their way through the slave quarters below as she continued to watch from the crack in the wall. She knew their voices, the sound of conquest and savagery. They were here again at the women's and children's quarters. On their way.

"Alright, go back to your business, we're not here for you," Master Martin Lewis said. "Mmmm, that stew sure smells good. Let me have a little bit of that in my tin cup," Lewis continued. "Dam. Goddam. That's good! I think you can teach old Mamie a few things. Looks like she might have lost her touch being up there in the big house so long," Lewis laughed as he continued his passage through the quarters.

"Holy shit! How old is that there gal?" a boisterous Winston Barksdale shouted.

The men were getting closer. Genevieve could smell the odor of the night ride and sweat of the horse manure mixed with the moonshine that breathed through the men's bodies.

"Did you hear me?" Winston shouted, "How old is that there gal?"

"My baby girl is only five years old, Master," Genevieve heard a woman answer.

"You wouldn't lie to me, would you? She looks to me to be a ripe, maybe twelve or thirteen years old," Winston continued as his hand moved to touch the girl.

"We need to keep our eyes on this one," Winston yelled to Martin who was just a few steps ahead of him.

The woman spoke-up again. "Master my baby is only five years old. She's no good to you Master. Take me instead."

Winston moved away from the girl. Then he glanced at the woman and then touched his private parts with a suggestive gesture but walked away.

"Come on Winston. Stay focused. We got to get to the girl," Martin said as he turned to see where Winston was.

The men kept moving forward while glancing around the quarters, lightly touching, smiling, nodding approval, and pointing at several of the younger girls as they passed them.

Genevieve could see the men were closer. The thumping sound of their boots through the last corner of the quarters and the undeniable stench was all too familiar. To reach her hiding place the men had to climb the wooden stairs and cross a small covered wooden landing. They had to be careful and pay attention not to fall through any loose planks.

She had a few minutes.

Waiting in the darkness, the quiet moment before defeat reminded Genevieve of the pit at the well on the other side of the plantation. She was placed or thrown there by her mother as a sacrifice during a black magic ceremony when she was eight years old. Somehow, she was saved by old lady Ma Hattie Harrison who found Genevieve at the bottom of the well and took care of her until she was able to be on her own. Genevieve never saw her mother again nor did she know what had happened to her.

She waited. She could hear them breathing. In her mind she could see old lady Ma Hattie standing there; ready to rescue her again. But there was no one standing there. Ma Hattie had saved her life. Old lady Harrison, a house slave who tried to teach Genevieve to read, somehow always found her. Genevieve didn't want to go but had no choice. When the master gave an order, you had to obey. That's what old lady Harrison and the other women slaves who worked the Barksdale and Lewis land taught the others. Genevieve knew each time her name was called she had to go. She understood what was ahead.

Martin's booming voice yelled out, "Slave girl, slave girl, no need to hide. Come on out here." He chuckled and repeated, "Slave girl, where are you?"

"She's over there!" Winston shouted, pointing to the corner near the straw bed where Genevieve had hidden several times before.

There really was nowhere to hide.

"She's the feisty one," Martin said, still laughing. "Come here, come here gal," he said as he reached for the zipper of his pants with one hand and grabbed Genevieve with the other. "Everyone knows you are my favorite."

The two men chained her up and took turns brutally raping her, something she had endured many times from the age of twelve. There was nothing she could do except to thrust her body back and forth the way she was taught would satisfy any man and hope it would all quickly come to an end. She silently called on the spirits of her ancestors to intervene and save her.

A black cat sat nearby, watching what was happening. Genevieve's and the cat's eyes met, and immediately Genevieve's energy was restored to withstand whatever was next. She thanked her ancestors for sending the cat as a sign that everything would be okay. She thought of the first time Master Lewis had raped her. He went into a kind of trance, talking about forgiveness, betrayal, and death while raping her. She would later learn a spell had been placed on him when he ate the stew from the woman in the slave quarters below.

When it was finally over, Genevieve's limp body fell on the bed. The men looked at Genevieve and she looked into both men's eyes—not something slaves were allowed to do. Martin Lewis and Winston Barksdale realized at that moment their lives had been changed forever.

"What the fuck is that black cat doing back in here?" Winston spouted.

Martin turned to look at the cat. He knew right away a black cat was not a good sign, particularly in slave quarters where black magic was regularly practiced. He knew something dark was about to happen. He could feel it. Had the slave girl cast a spell on him?

"Let's get out of here," Winston said as he grabbed his hat and belt. "Let's just go." Martin reached for the collar and chains from underneath Genevieve's body as he kneeled closer and whispered, "I'll be back for you."

Genevieve lay there thinking how one day she would destroy these men and their families and everything they touched. Somehow, she had to stay alive long enough to get her revenge.

The stories the slaves shared with each other about what had happened on the other plantations began to flood her mind with ideas. She remembered the letters Ma Hattie read out loud to the other slaves about fights between the slaves and the owners regarding freedom and how the slave women were treated. She thought about the stories she heard about slave revolts and uprisings on the other plantations in Louisiana. She thought about the burning corpses at the black magic ceremony when she was a child, how she would sneak away to the back woods and watch the slaves from the Haitian tribes practice voodoo. More than ever, right now Genevieve knew she wanted to learn the secrets of voodoo. She would learn the black magic of her ancestors to get her revenge and invoke a curse on Masters Martin Lewis and Winston Barksdale.

The cat returned and jumped up alongside Genevieve onto the bed. He sat there staring at something on the other side of the room. Genevieve was exhausted, almost too sore to turn her head. She needed to follow the cat's glaring eyes to see what the cat was looking at.

Something fell. Genevieve turned to look.

She saw the doll and a man's sock on the floor. The doll belonged to the little Barksdale girl. She had seen the girl with the doll last summer as she stepped out of the carriage while visiting the Lewis plantation. Genevieve remembered that summer well because she heard the little girl screaming from a room in the back of the big house. She also saw Lewis Martin leave the house later after the screaming stopped. Genevieve never saw the Barksdale girl at the planation again after that visit. Genevieve looked around the room trying to follow the cat's gaze through her swollen eyes.

The cat jumped off the bed and stared down at something on the floor. The cat pulled a large brown pouch from under the bed that one of the men had left behind. Genevieve was so weak and could hardly move, she knew better than to steal anything. They would hang her for stealing, but she was curious about what was inside the pouch.

Slowly she moved her aching body off the bed to the floor. Her insides were on fire and burning with pain, her hands sore and fingers swollen from the chains, her eyes blurry and heavy. She felt for the pouch and began to slowly open it.

Genevieve knew she had to hurry since the men would certainly recognize they had left something behind; hopefully, they would fall asleep in the woods somewhere, exhausted from their conquest, and drink themselves into a deep sleep before realizing the pouch was missing and begin to back-track to recover it.

Inside the pouch she felt something wrapped loosely with a cotton cloth. Then she looked more closely and realized there were photographs inside the wrapping. She couldn't see well enough to make out the people in the pictures, so she placed them back into the pouch and searched for what else might be inside. She found loose coins, tobacco, and lots of papers with writing and stamps. Nothing seemed particularly important.

She heard hissing and growling from the cat. The cat turned away from Genevieve's side and ran under a large closet with a mirror that sat exactly across the room from where the dresser sat in the otherwise sparsely furnished room. The room was named "the black magic room" by the Haitian slave women because it was where they practiced witchcraft, conducted meetings and met in private to maintain their customs.

Genevieve tried to pick her body up to get back on the bed, but she just didn't have the strength. Afraid the two men were returning; she pushed the opened pouch under the low-hanging bed frame and pretended she was dead on the floor.

The door opened.

"Lord have mercy! Did they kill this here gal? What did they do? Poor child," the voices repeated, "Lord have mercy, Oh my god. What did they do?" Genevieve recognized the voices. The voices were the women slaves who occupied the slave quarters with her.

"Thank you, Jesus. I believe the gal is alive," someone said. "See? She's breathing."

"Genevieve, Genevieve can you hear me? It's me, Ma Hattie. Are you alive? Are you alive child?"

Seconds passed. Nothing. The room was quiet. The cat lay under an old mahogany mirrored closet watching the women. He too was afraid. Perhaps he had witnessed too many animal sacrifices on the plantation. The cat tried to stay out of their path.

Slowly the women heard Genevieve's voice.

"I ain't dead yet," Genevieve said in a slow whispering voice. She tried to open her eyes, but they were so swollen it was difficult to know for sure whether or not they were open.

Sitting on the floor next to Genevieve was the old woman named Ma Hattie Harrison. It was said she had special powers that had saved many slaves from their deaths. Most people feared the old woman because of her powers and seeming influence over the white slave owners.

"Okay, you be still, child. We are here now and are going to take care of you," Ma Hattie said. "Be still and quiet, we're here."

Three other women had accompanied Ma Hattie to the room, their craft was not as godly as Ma Hattie's. The three women were from Haiti, and they came from a culture that practiced voodoo and witchcraft. It was all these women ever knew until they met the spiritual Ma Hattie. She was from Ghana. Genevieve too was a descendant of the Haitian-born slaves. She was separated from her kin folk and bought to Louisiana on a ship with just her mother and other Haitian girls and women when she was six years old. She had lived on the Lewis plantation ever since.

The three women were angry and getting angrier as they saw Genevieve's battered and bloodied body. The mattress on the bed above heavily stained with a mixture of blood and semen, the welts across Genevieve's thighs, her swollen eyes and face, and chain marks around her wrists were gut-wrenching to see. Unfortunately, the women had all experienced similar horrors. They were reminded of their own rapes and the public lashings of other slave women they had witnessed during their lifetime on the Lewis plantation. The site of burn marks down Genevieve's inner thighs from the hot oil the men had used for lubrication bought tears to the women's eyes, for they too had experienced the same fate with the Lewis and Barksdale boys when they were younger.

The women's anger turned into rage and a desire for revenge. The women spoke amongst themselves about helping the girl get her revenge on the men. They called it Genevieve's curse.

Looking up at the women, Ma Hattie paused, realizing they were up to something. Ma Hattie was gifted with strong intuition, and she feared the women would try to coax the girl to put a spell on the men in revenge. She needed to protect the girl as best as she could.

"Help me get this girl up on the bed," Ma Hattie instructed.

The women lifted Genevieve onto the bed. The touch of her naked and wounded body sparked a deep feeling of vengeance in their souls.

"Chatty," said Ma Hattie, "go get some hot water and Velma go get that castile soap, Lucy you go fetch that rubbing oil and herbs from Mrs. Mammie. Tell her I sent you." She looked at each of the women as she assigned their tasks. "Carrie, go over to the big house, knock twice on the back door, wait a little bit, then knock three more times very lightly. Ask old Sam for some hot food for the girl. Tell him I sent you. Now you be careful. I'll stay and pray with Genevieve until you each return." Ma Hattie walked the women to the door.

Ma Hattie grabbed an old blanket sitting on the windowsill. She looked out the window. Genevieve could see the old woman standing there clutching the blanket; then she began to gather Genevieve's clothes that had been scattered about the room. She sighed as she looked down at Genevieve.

The black cat came out of his hiding place and sat next to Ma Hattie and with a purr rubbed his face into her dress. She sat down at the edge of the broken-down bed and began to pray. Genevieve began to fall asleep, lulled by the rhythm of Ma Hattie's prayers.

A few hours had passed before the women were all together again. When they arrived in the room, they saw the cat lying next to Ma Hattie, who appeared to be asleep. The girl's eyes were so swollen it was difficult to tell for sure if she was awake or asleep. The women had discussed amongst themselves the ways Genevieve could get revenge. They just needed time alone with her without Ma Hattie in the room. They decided one of them would volunteer to spend the night with the girl and then they would all come back and talk with the girl about their plan.

"Ma Hattie, Ma Hattie, wake up," Chatty said as she gently shook the old woman.

The cat began to hiss at the women, and they slowly backed away.

"You're back? Good! What took you so long?" Ma Hattie said, standing. "Let's get this girl cleaned up. Did you bring my herbs?"

Ma Hattie noticed the cat looked frightened and was hissing. Where did the cat come from? Why was he there? Then she realized the cat was there to protect Genevieve. She was in danger.

"Ma Hattie," a cautious Chatty began. "I can stay with the girl the rest of tonight before I need to get to Master's house in the morning. Why don't you go and get some rest? We can take care of the girl."

Genevieve heard the women talking and she slowly reached for Ma Hattie's hand and held it tight.

"No, I'll stay with the girl and clean her up. You all go and get some sleep. You need to be in the fields tomorrow morning," said Ma Hattie with suspicion.

Lucy started to say something but Chatty and Velma held her arm. The women all turned and walked out of the room.

"Ma Hattie, why didn't you let them stay with me?" Genevieve asked.

"Oh child, sometimes you just get a feeling about things. God blessed me with getting that feeling." Ma Hattie smiled and began to wash the child's body.

Genevieve grimaced in pain as the cloth touched her skin, and Ma Hattie shushed her, telling her it would be okay. But Ma Hattie knew the girl was not safe. As she carefully tended to her, she decided to move the girl to her quarters and take care of her until she was strong enough to be back on her own. She would work with old Nate the overseer to get the girl some lighter chores while she healed.

The weeks passed quickly, and Genevieve recovered, but something was still wrong. She was suddenly finding herself tired and unable to eat without feeling sick. Genevieve hadn't gotten her period and she feared she might be with child and the father was one of the men who had raped her. If so, she would never have the child. She had to see Ma Hattie, but her rescuer had taken ill suddenly. The rumor was someone had tried to work roots on her and Ma Hattie found out and broke the spell.

"I think I'm with child," Genevieve confided in Chatty who was in her early thirties and had befriended Genevieve shortly after the rape and her return to the cotton fields.

"One of them?" Chatty said as she nodded toward the big house.

"I don't know which one," Genevieve said. "Either way, I don't want this baby. I will never love it." "We all got babies around here from these white men and we don't always know who their daddy is. But we still love our babies. It's not their fault how they got here."

"I hate what's in my stomach and I will never love it," Genevieve said more quietly. "I hate Master Lewis and I hate Master Barksdale. I probably hate Master Lewis more." She looked up at the big house. "Them two white men are the only men I ever been with. Loving their baby would be impossible. I wish my baby would die. I will never love it."

"Never say never. You don't know what you'll do given the circumstances. This will be your first one and the first one is special. You will love it. You are just afraid. Give it time, Genevieve," Chatty said as she fixed her eyes on Genevieve with a frown of knowing disgust.

The women finished their chores and headed for the wagon to hand over their pickings for the day. Afterward, they walked back to the women's slave quarters in silence.

Genevieve sat on the straw bed on her side of the slave quarters alone and frightened. She had no one to talk to. She looked out through the cracks of the shed at the big house. She would wait for the lights to go out and then she would meet Chatty at the black magic room that night.

The door was partially open, and emanating from the room was the familiar smell, like burned flesh. But Genevieve knew it was from the flowers that grew on the other side of the cotton field near the big house. But there was also something else. It was the smell of death. She remembered it accompanying the dead bodies and animals back home.

The room was lit with small candles and lanterns, the windows covered with a black cloth. The dresser had been turned on its side, making it into a table. She walked closer to the table that stood right in front of the room, a large book sat in the center, and other ornaments unfamiliar to Genevieve decorated the room. A gold tin cup was on the table filled with a dark red liquid. At the same time the odor in the room began to turn her stomach, she noticed the remains of the black cat.

Standing in a circle around her now were the women, some dressed in black and others in white. A chair had been placed in the middle of the circle. She could see the bed where she had been raped was now covered with a beautiful white cloth, fresh lily flowers framing its edges. There was a large red rug on the floor and another chair was placed on the rug next to the bed.

"Sit down child," an unfamiliar voice ordered in a matter-of-fact manner. "We are here to help you get your revenge."

Genevieve walked over and sat in the high-backed chair covered with a black cloth embossed with the familiar signs: circles representing the sprits she was taught to call on to place a spell or curse on others. She had never wanted to use her powers until now. For just a fleeting moment she thought about Ma Hattie and the Harrison slaves. They worshipped a different spirit and were different from anyone she ever knew. Whatever she did next, she wouldn't do anything to hurt the Harrison descendants.

"We're here to help our daughter and sister reclaim her birthright," began a strange voice. "To claim the powers she's entitled, to curse and cast a spell upon the men of the Lewis and Barksdale families to pay for the sins of their forefathers, Master Martin Lewis and Master Winston Barksdale.

The group of women spoke in unison words that were not clear to Genevieve. The women held their hands together over their heads as they chanted the unfamiliar words. The aroma from the candles and smoke from the handmade pipes that filled the room and the chanting put Genevieve in a trance-like state. She turned toward the bed. The brown pouch she had tucked under the bed months ago was now lying at the foot of the bed. The pictures she could not see clearly the night she was raped were posted on the wall behind the bed. She could not see the pictures clearly now because of the darkness of the room. The doll and sock she saw that same night were next to the pouch.

In a trance Genevieve walked over to the wall. She saw the faces of the pictures that were in the pouch: Master

Winston Barksdale, his wife, a little boy, and a baby in Mrs. Barksdale's arms. The second photo was a picture of the Lewis plantation with the Big House in the background. The third picture on the wall was Master Martin Lewis, his pregnant wife, and two little girls holding the doll that now sat at the bottom of the bed.

"Genevieve, we are here tonight to help you get your revenge on those who have caused you great pain and suffering. What do you wish?" the woman spoke.

Genevieve replied, "Generations will experience troubled minds. There will be mistrust and betrayal between each other in all their dealings. The men folk will never hold onto love, and the men's lives will end in tragedy. The same fate I wish for my unborn child and the descendants of this unwanted and devil-conceived birth."

The women helped Genevieve to lay down on the bed. The doll and pictures were then set on fire. As the women watched and Genevieve smiled beyond the pain she felt in her womb. Was it a sign of some sort?

Suddenly the door flew open. Ma Hattie stood there, dressed in white with a cross.

Ma Hattie walked over to the bed where Genevieve was as the women began to back away into the corners of the room. They knew the powers of this woman and they were afraid.

"You have done a terrible, terrible, terrible thing," Ma Hattie said to the women.

"You have destroyed the lives of so many, and now Genevieve will carry this child who no one wants, a child with no name and no home." Ma Hattie stopped talking when she heard the scream. The other women came closer to the bed.

"Get it out of me! Get it out of me!" an agonizing, sweating, and shivering Genevieve screamed as she took her fists and hit herself in the stomach. "Get this thing out! Get out! I hate you!"

"You'll be okay baby, you'll be okay. It's the devil working inside of you, not your baby," Ma Hattie said as she tried to grab Genevieve's fists. The other women looked on, unsure what to do or say. So, they began to return the room back to its original state.

Ma Hattie placed her hands on Genevieve's stomach and began to pray, while rubbing it in various rhythmic motions. Soon the pain was gone.

The room was quiet. The women were at the door about to leave when Ma Hattie stood.

"Stop!" Ma Hattie began. "You have done something me and my people do not practice. We believe in other spirits. We believe our power is greater than yours, but I know you have powers I do not have. I've prayed that redemption will come to these families and the descendants born to the child inside Genevieve's womb. The answer I received is that redemption will only come through a Harrison descendant… my descendant. The child's powers and gifts will be greater than all ours together. That person will be a woman who will change the destiny of many.

Ma Hattie paused for a few moments, then said, "We will speak of this night to no one, but we will write down the redemption vision so that later generations will know it's possible to reverse a curse."

The women left the room without a word.

Genevieve sat up on the bed and swept the ashes and remains from the burnt doll and sock into the pouch. Ma Hattie watched the girl closely, realizing the black magic and other spirit worship that happened this night was just the beginning for this slave girl named Genevieve.

Chapter 2

The Windowsill

Harrisburg, Pennsylvania, Fall 1952

Kizzy ran as fast as she could. The weight of fear clutched her tiny body and thoughts of surrender occupied her mind. She imagined she was a puppet like the one she had just played with in her kindergarten class earlier in the day, only this was different. Now someone else was pulling the strings and doing the talking. Kizzy was confused, wondering whether she was awake or if this was one of her dreams. She kept running. It started days after Kizzy witnessed the dog Old Pal eating Miss Sally, the lady from down the street.

She continued to run ahead of the other kids, thinking she could trick Old Pal. If she was alone, the dog might not notice her because he seemed to bark at the kids when he heard them laughing and playing whenever they passed by the house he guarded like a solider at war.

Kizzy was almost there. *Just a few more steps.* The Caldwell house was a simple green and white wood-framed two-story house built during the war. There was a huge picture window in the front of the house, and three slabs of concrete for steps. The door frame was wood and painted a dark green. Three windows upstairs and the one large window downstairs were covered with white Venetian blinds. The Caldwell house was next to an alley on one side and Katz's grocery store was on the other side. Kizzy and her youngest brother Vincent would watch the rats crawl over the fruits and vegetables every night. They lived right across the street from the alley where Old Pal lived. Kiz had figured out how to trick the old dog and understood his moods. She had watched him from the window every day, and around 3:30 pm Kizzy would run the three blocks from Cumberland to 7th and 7th to Cumberland streets.

For some reason, Kizzy wasn't afraid of Old Pal. Even at seven years old, she seemed to understand the streets that engulfed her life, the people, the sounds, the smells. She had no way to express herself then, but the street and neighborhood where she came from allowed her to breathe. She felt protected but did not understand why at the time. Kizzy could feel the heaviness lift from her body, she could finally breathe, she was safe, and she was now home.

"Goodbye Mr. Pal. I'll see you later," Kizzy yelled at the old dog. As if on cue, the old dog barked twice.

Kizzy ran up the crushed and broken concrete steps. "One, two, three, four," she counted out loud as she skipped up the steps. She gripped the doorknob and tried to turn it, but it didn't open. She shoved her small body with all the force she had to get inside the house.

She began to get frustrated with the door. *Okay*, she thought to herself, *push hard*. She recalled watching her brothers and sisters pushing their shoulders into the door then using their feet and shoulders at the same time against the door, so she leaned forward and did the same things. She smiled thinking that what she learned from her siblings, she did better.

"Okay, okay, Kizzy, I'm not going to tell you again. Stop pushing against the door! You are going to hurt yourself one of these days," said Larry, the oldest of Kizzy's three brothers, mimicking the voice of their dad, who was at work. He had ordered all the kids to stop pushing against the door. Larry continued mocking his dad: "One of these days you are going to break that door." Kizzy laughed, as did Larry as he opened the door, for Kizzy had failed and fallen to the floor.

"Are you okay?" Larry asked, still amused by mocking his dad.

"Yeah," Kizzy said. She had scratched her knee, but she was old enough to know a knee scratch was nothing. No one cared. Plus, she did not want to be called a crybaby and get Larry in trouble.

"Is everybody okay out there? What's that commotion? Larry, what are you up to, boy!" their mother called out.

"Nothing, Mom, just Kizzy coming home. I was opening the door for her," Larry said. He then glanced over at Kizzy as if to say, *keep your mouth shut, this is our secret!*

"Kizzy, you all right?" their mom yelled from the kitchen.

"I'm okay, Mommy," Kizzy said as she approached the kitchen where her mom was starting dinner.

"Okay, give me a kiss, then."

Kiz leaned over to give her mom a big kiss and hug.

"Now, go upstairs, change your clothes, and take a nap. Alice will wake you up when it's time for dinner." Alice was the oldest of Kizzy's two older sisters.

"Okay, Mommy," Kiz said as she turned toward the steps and hit her sore knee on the kitchen entry jamb. "Ouch!" she yelled as blood trickled down her leg.

"Kizzy, what happened?" her mom asked.

"Nothing. I fell at school and hurt my knee," Kizzy said as she reached for the towel her mom held out to her.

"Okay, now you go ahead and get some rest," Kizzy's mom said, shaking her head.

Kizzy was always in a hurry, stumbling as she ran up the steps. Mrs. Caldwell watched her little girl rush up the steps and wondered, as she had done so many times, why the child was always running. Was she running to something or from something?

Emily Caldwell's thoughts about Kizzy were perplexed. She always felt Kizzy was different from her other children and needed more from her than she could give. Even now at just seven years old, a distance in the relationship between mother and daughter had developed. Emily wanted to give Kizzy the world, she just didn't know how.

What she did know is she had to protect this child. She paused a moment at the bottom of the staircase as she listened to Kizzy moved around restlessly above her. She knew it would be just a matter of time before the creaking sound of the child opening the window would happen. What did the child see when she looked out the window? Did she see the world as it is or did she see something else? She worried about Kizzy, her youngest daughter. Hopefully she'd find time to write in her journal, which was how she worked things out that troubled her.

The Caldwells were a happy family, and the young kids enjoyed the security of good parents who did their best to provide for the young kids, or at least the best they knew how.

Emily Harrison Caldwell was married at sixteen years old to Brownie Caldwell when he was nineteen years old. They were both from Macon, Georgia and both of them had a high school education. Colored folks from the South respected education. It was a high priority and considered important and highly valued for the poor kids whose parents were direct descendants of slavery.

Both the Harrison and Caldwell families who lived in Georgia were disappointed when Emily and Brownie decided to get married and move north. They moved north to live with older relatives who had left the South after the Civil War and never returned. Both the Harrison and Caldwell families were considered lower-class, uneducated colored folks from the South. Because Emily and Brownie had good-paying jobs, steady work, and were church folks, they were accepted into the community, a community they created for themselves with others whose backgrounds were similar to their own.

When Emily was fifteen years old, she started keeping a journal. Her mother (Grandma Mamie) would bring her scrap paper from the Graceland and Glory paper mill where she worked. Emily's grandparents were once slaves on the Grace and Glory cotton plantation adjacent to the mill. Emily's great-great-grandma was Ma Hattie Harrison.

Grandma Mamie would tell Emily stories about her life as a slave, what a "strong woman" meant, and the importance of keeping a record of who you are so you can share it with your children and their children. Emily would try to capture her grandma's words in her journal.

"What you got on that there paper?" Grandma Mamie would ask a young Emily.

"Just a few words about my day, Grandma," Emily would respond.

"Okay, gal. One of these days you are going to read to me what you wrote on that there paper. You're educated and I'm proud of that, but I want to hear you speak. I want to hear your voice. Don't just hide behind those words on that paper. Not everybody is going to understand those words. I want you to write them words and speak them, just like you were telling me a story." Emily Caldwell thought a lot about her conversations with her grandmother and tried hard to write things down to share with her future family.

She would carefully stash her writings under the floorboard in the farmhouse where she lived then with the intent of never sharing them with anyone other than her future family. The writings were just her private thoughts; a way to control her frustrations and a way to cry without anyone seeing her tears.

One evening in 1934, as she was walking down an old country road with some of the other kids who attended the one-room schoolhouse, she noticed an old woman sitting on the side of the road. The woman had her face in her lap. She wore a white cotton dress, sandals, long beads, and earrings. Her long, dark curly hair hung like a protective scarf from the glaring rays of sun illuminating the road. She was covered all over with red Georgia dirt.

The kids all called her a witch. Emily walked closer. She was curious to know more about this woman who sat on the edge of the road every day and said nothing to anybody. No one saw her face, and no one seem to know her name or where she was from. Emily and the other kids didn't remember her being there during the previous school year, nor did they see her anywhere else in town.

As Emily approached the woman, she felt a distinct surge go through her body for just a second. *Whoa, what was that?* She stopped.

"You have finally come. Sit here beside me," the woman said as she lifted her head from her lap and looked up at Emily. "Don't be afraid. I'm here to deliver a message to you."

Emily was terrified and curious at the same. She couldn't move.

"Don't be afraid," the woman said. "I was sent here to tell you a secret."

"Who are you?" Emily asked as she looked around for the others, wondering where everyone went and how she ended up alone on the side of the road with the mystery woman. Emily also felt like something was happening to her body. She was tingling all over.

"Calm down child," the woman said as she stood and walked a few steps in front of Emily.

Emily was stunned and almost hypnotized. The figure in front of her was neither female nor male, and the hair flowed across what would have been a face, but she could only see a hollow space. Somehow, the fear Emily felt just moments earlier had dissipated. She was in awe of this figure in front of her and felt something special was about to happen to her. "Who are you?" Emily asked again as the tingling in her body went away.

"My name is the name given to me by those I watch over," The figure said.

"I don't understand," Emily responded.

The figure continued, "You will one day remember this encounter. Your yet-to-be-born daughter will know my name. Your child will be blessed, although her life will be filled with tests, challenges, and opportunities. She will experience betrayal, pain, love, loss, and enormous success. She has a particular destiny to fulfill. You will become one of her sacrifices. Let her know you forgive her. You'll know when the time is right to share this with her."

"Please help me. I don't understand. I don't have any kids. I'm only fifteen years old," Emily said.

"You'll have many children. They will all be special to you as a mother, but the little girl will be your blessed one. Leave her with this message when she's old enough to understand."

A swirl of dust encircled Emily as the figure disappeared.

"Emily, Emily, wake up! Wake up!"

Emily was lying in the middle of the old country road covered with dust with a small white feather next to her side.

"What happened?" Brownie Caldwell asked. Several other kids from the schoolhouse gathered around Emily too.

"The old lady…" Emily started, but then she noticed the other kids looking at her with a strange stare.

"What old lady?" asked Brownie.

"The lady… she was sitting right here… next to me," Emily said as she looked past Brownie and down the road.

"There is no one else here, Emily. Are you okay?" Brownie asked in a worried voice. "We've been looking for you for a few hours."

Emily realized she had experienced something unusual. "Where am I?"

Brownie continued, "You are on the country road on the other side of the abandoned Baptist church."

As the other kids began to go back down the hill after seeing she was safe and okay, they chattered about the heat and how Emily probably had a heat stroke or something.

No one could figure out why she had gone alone to the old country road near the abandoned church. Was she going to meet someone? If so, who? The kids all laughed and walked on home.

Brownie looked at Emily as he helped her stand up. He too was curious as he watched her staring at the abandoned church.

"Emily, are you ready to go?" he asked.

Emily turned and looked Brownie right in the face. "When we get married, we'll have a church three times the size of this old, abandoned church. But we'll have to find a way to keep the devil out."

After Emily got home, she reached for her journal and wrote down everything she experienced. Then she decided to write a special message to her unborn future daughter:

My Special Daughter,

You are reading this letter because you have been chosen as one of seven people who will change the world. I do not know how. You were born with something others will want and need for power and redemption. I don't understand it. I am so afraid for you. A woman told me you will be in great danger throughout your life. You will experience life to the fullest, with love, betrayal, sorrow, and moments of happiness and much success. The woman promised me you would have the protection of our ancestors. You will be the builder of something great my dear daughter. My death will be one of your greatest sorrows. Please do not blame yourself. My death will be my sacrifice to ensure you fulfill your destiny. I look forward to meeting you. One day you'll understand everything. Meanwhile, I'll keep writing.

Your mother, Emily

Harrisburg, Pennsylvania, 1951

Emily and Brownie got married a few years later and left Georgia. When she and Brownie left Georgia in 1938, the first thing she remembered to bring with her was the writing book. Why she was thinking of that book now caused her to pause a minute. She had not written a word since March 12, 1945, two days after Kizzy was born. Emily decided to start writing again. It was now clear to her that Kizzy was the special daughter.

She decided to start writing between preparing dinner and waiting for the other kids to come home. She would continue to write late at night while Brownie was with the men and the kids were sleeping. The house would be quiet then.

Kizzy woke up from her nap around 5:30 pm to the smell of baked macaroni and fried chicken, as well as loud arguments amongst her older siblings about who was the smartest and who would be famous. She could hear Uncle Bennie's unique voice, always sounding like he was about to scream at you, and the radio played softly in the background.

Emily Caldwell loved music of all kinds. Although she was a Christian woman, she kept the blues on all day until Brownie came home.

Emily Caldwell would tell the kids, "Go turn on Bandstand." The kids loved the music too, and somehow, they all knew the music from the juke joint across the street and on the radio, even though it was not allowed in their house. Bandstand was off-limits too when their dad was home.

Kizzy enjoyed the activities inside the house but mostly enjoyed what was happening outside. After dinner, she would go upstairs and sit on the windowsill in her bedroom, watching and listening to the activity outside. Friday and Saturday nights were her favorite time to eavesdrop on the people who visited the streets surrounding her house. She would stay at the window until her oldest sister Alice called her to come downstairs for dinner.

Friday and Saturday nights people crowded the narrow streets between Cumberland, Calder, 6th, and 7th. Kizzy would open the window and listen to car horns blowing, music blasting from the corner bar, a mixture of laugher and quiet conversation from people walking along the streets, and men and women holding each other's hands. Often, she would spot a couple in the alley kissing or having sex, the drunks would stumble out of the corner bar, sometimes looking for trouble, other times appearing to want to be alone. She would see men dressed up as women and women kissing other women. The foul language she heard no child should have ever been exposed to, but Kizzy was.

The night sky held the promise of escape for the little girl who sat on the windowsill. Each star she could see gave her hope there were more. When the stars could not be seen, she would look for the moon or some other object the naked eye might not see.

Then there was the dog Old Pal whose occasional bark for no reason in her direction signaled to Kizzy he knew she was there. Kizzy would pick up a shoe and tap it two times to signal to Old Pal she heard him. He would bark back two times in acknowledgment. The two of them found other ways to communicate that confirmed Kiz's feelings that Old Pal was more than just an old dog.

She continued to survey the street when she saw two men with knives and another with a gun cursing and threatening each other about a gambling debt. As the men staggered toward each other, a small crowd from the bar and candy store surrounded them.

Kizzy began to yawn. She had seen this scene so many times before, but she couldn't go to sleep until she saw who the woman in the blue and white car was. Did the woman know that other women who entered the blue and white car never returned? Would she be different?

Kizzy started to drift off to sleep when the music from the juke joint filled her ears and made her sway from side to side. The music was coming from the juke joint on James and Calder streets. The music made her feel a particular way. She couldn't quite describe it then, but later she would understand it was called "the blues." As the juke joint music became stronger, she could hear the voice of Rev. Dinkins in the distance, the church not far away. Rev. Richard Dinkins always talked about sinners. The people she saw every day on the street where she lived—the drunks, the cursing words, the women with red lipstick, the smell of old perfume, and tight dresses—were these Rev. Dinkins' sinners? Why Rev. Dinkins didn't like these people the little girl tried hard to understand. These people were nice to her. She saw them every morning. They gave her books to read, candy, and big smiles. Sometimes she would get advice from Rev. Dinkins' sinners, such as, "Child you get up and get out of here and make something of yourself. Don't be like me," or "Go to college, get yourself a good job," or "Find yourself a nice, educated man to take care of you," or "Don't depend on nobody for nothing." Kizzy would get advice almost every day from Miss Sally.

The only thing she knew then was she did not want to be like any of them, but she knew nothing else, except her mom, dad, uncles, and the other people from her church. They were different, although she never quite understood how different.

Kizzy closed her eyes, hoping to drown out the commotions of the typical weekend night in the neighborhood. The music and shouting sounds seemed to get louder and were coming from the Pentecostal church a few blocks away. Later she could hear men's voices coming closer, their voices recognizable although muddled. She heard them but did not understand what they were saying. She tried hard to listen with her eyes closed. Years later, she would understand what they were saying. She was just a child when she first started listening to the men who gathered at night at her house.

Kizzy had a secret nobody knew she had. If she told it, she didn't think anyone would believe her, so she kept it to herself. Kizzy didn't know her mom knew her secret.

Spring 1952, Brownie Caldwell

Brownie Caldwell had a good paying job working for the railroad and a second job working at the steel mill. The only time the kids would see their father was at night between jobs.

Kizzy would peek out of the window late at night, waiting for her father to come home. She would wait to see him park the old red and white Buick in the space reserved for him in front of the house, then she would tiptoe from the bedroom she shared with her two sisters down the hall to the top of the stairway where she would situate herself on the very top step, in clear view for him to see her as he opened the door.

Six days a week, Brownie Caldwell would open the door and do a quick peek-a-boo with Kizzy before dashing off to the back washroom with the old washing machine to clean some of the dirt off from the mill. He did not want his kids to see him come home with dirt all over him. Fully satisfied, Kizzy would tiptoe back to the bedroom and fall into a deep sleep and wake up five hours later to greet her dad in the morning before he left for his next job at 6:00 am.

After washing up, Brownie Caldwell would sit alone at the kitchen table. On this particular night, he was thinking about the conversation the men had earlier at the union hall. They all wanted to buy houses and send their kids to college so they could become the bosses and foremen they wanted their fathers to be. He often wondered if things would ever change for his family. He couldn't stand the thought of his boys working at the mill and on the railroad like he did. The disrespect the men encountered, whether black or white, was not what they wanted for their kids. Most of the men worked so hard because of their families. And yet, in many cases generations had been working at the mill. It was still one of the best jobs an uneducated man could hold, and some educated men too.

Brownie's heart broke every night when he saw little Kiz sitting on the top of the staircase. He had a difficult time looking at the child. He loved the little girl so much and could not bear the thoughts that crossed his mind when he would see her night after night on the top of the staircase waiting for him to come home. He thought even then that what she saw in him was not good. He thought she deserved more. The knocking at the door let him know the men from his union had arrived. He would go upstairs first to make sure everyone was okay, put Kizzy to bed, and give Emily a quick kiss, listen to her complaints about their sons and the new friends they were hanging around with, her day cleaning at the hotels, and of course Kizzy and how she worried something is wrong with the child. Brownie would reassure Emily

34

everything was okay. The kids are just growing and that's what kids do.

"One of these days I'm going to buy you one of those big houses uptown and you will never have to work again," he would always tell her.

Emily would give him an extra hug and kiss, and he would quickly refrain from going further, knowing he had a house full of men waiting for him downstairs.

So, he winked at Emily and whispered in her ear, "Keep the bed warm. I'll be back up in an hour. I got to take care of a little business downstairs."

Emily just looked at him and as he left the room, she leaned over to crack the splinter-infested window. As the cool night breeze blew softly across her face, she could sense the flickers of the chipped paint from the window's wooden casing falling in rhythm with the night and the chatter and noise from the street below. Rage, disappointment, and sadness were the only words to describe what she saw in Brownie's eyes that night. He was a proud and good man, but that was not enough for either of them.

As Brownie Caldwell closed the door to their bedroom, he asked himself, *What else can I do?* He walked a few steps to the two adjoining rooms to check on the boys first. They were okay. He knew they were just pretending to be asleep. He walked in and sat on the edge of the torn mattress. You could see the springs ready to pop any minute with just the right amount of pressure. Brownie told the boys to sit up.

"Boys, you are going to be men one day and you need to start thinking about that now. In life, you can either take a left or right turn. You'll need to decide. Whatever you decide, just make sure to make me and your mom proud. You'll make some mistakes along the way, so support each other, learn from each other, and know that God has each of you here for a reason. The sooner you know what that is the better off you'll be. Now listen to your mom. Goodnight and I'll see you tomorrow after work."

Of the three sons, Larry was the oldest at seventeen, Leon was fourteen, and Vincent was the youngest boy at eight years old. The older boys looked at each other wondering what their father had heard. Did he know about little Colin Rankin? The boys closed their eyes and fell into their own thoughts about what and how much their father knew about Colin Rankin. The last time he talked to them was about secrets. They heard him call out, then knock softly on the girls' bedroom door. Alice was the oldest at eighteen, Carmen was next at sixteen, and Kiz was the youngest, just seven years old at the time.

Brownie Caldwell poked his head into the girls' room and asked, "Is everything okay?"

Alice always replied for the girls. "Yeah, we are okay, Daddy. Everything is fine."

He smiled. "Okay, goodnight," he said and then closed the door.

Brownie Caldwell went downstairs to the kitchen and finished the dinner that had been placed in the oven for him. He waited for all the men to gather. Brownie was a reasonable man and considered a man's man. He was always in closed-door conversations with the men from church, neighborhood, and others whose voices Kizzy did not recognize. She would perch herself on the middle steps of the back staircase that curved into the kitchen and listen to the men. No one would see her there.

Alice continued to flip through the pages of the magazine her mom had brought home from the hotel after her dad closed the door. Alice loved looking at the beautiful women with their jewelry and clothes. She wondered if she could get a part-time job at Rankin's department store downtown and go to secretarial school after graduation. She would talk with her mom first.

Carmen was thinking about the boy she saw today at the candy store. He smiled and waved at her. She waved back. She wondered where he lived and why was he at the candy store. She thought she had seen him before, but she could not remember where. Maybe he attended the new integrated junior high school to which the colored kids from the eighth ward had been reassigned. She would later learn his name was Kyle Jason Rankin, III, and he attended the prestigious Jewish school in town.

Kizzy pretended to be asleep while she waited for Alice to click off the dim lamp. Carmen would fall asleep immediately, and Alice wouldn't be too far behind. All of the Caldwell children were great sleepers except for Kizzy. She was a lot like her dad in that regard, and she was proud of it. She waited for the girls to go to sleep.

Quiet as a mouse, she snuck over to the window and slowly opened it. This was her special spot. She sat in the window, perched on the sill to get a good look at the outside, the palms of her hands cupping her face and her shoulder hunched over to help hold up the old window. Her piercing dark eyes were wide open, lips tightly closed, legs at an angle to give her body the support she needed to see everything. What she saw on a daily basis was craziness, yet this was her reality, although she knew even then there was something different for her and this was not where she was meant to be. Chips from the old grey paint would occasionally peel off the wood frame and fall on her dark skin. The old window was broken, of course, like everything else in that old house and neighborhood.

Kiz Lamise Caldwell

As a young child they called her Kizzy, she called herself Kiz Lamise Caldwell or KLC and by the time she became a teenager, everyone called her by her proper full name, Kiz Lamise Caldwell. As far back as people can remember, KLC was considered smart, independent, sophisticated, disciplined, beautiful, and sad. KLC would have described herself the same way.

KLC was born on March 10, 1945, at Harrisburg Hospital in Harrisburg, Pennsylvania. She was the youngest of the six children born to Brownie and Emily Caldwell. It was rumored that KLC was taken from her mother's arms by a nurse who was smitten by the child's beauty. The nurse carried the newborn throughout the hospital for other staff to see the beautiful Caldwell baby. People said KLC was rescued by a strange man (no one could ever agree who) who took the newborn from the nurse to a waiting station for new fathers and handed the baby to her father. Brownie would later say he thought the man was one of the doctors, although he too could not describe the man. The incident was forgotten, but KLC would hear the same story about the nurse and doctor throughout her childhood.

Kiz Lamise Caldwell was a stunningly beautiful child: milk chocolate skin, big dark brown eyes, a petite body frame and thick black hair. Even as a child she was always well groomed. She learned the art of style and grooming from her sister Alice, who she admired. KLC was a very particular child with a vivid imagination.

By the time KLC was seven years old, she had seen and experienced more things than most people would experience in their lifetime. Ah, there he goes again; the mystery man that haunted her dreams and showed up in her private thoughts. He seemed to know where to find her either in her dreams or her quiet place. He was like a shadow, a blur. She never really saw his face, just an image that would appear with projections of contradictions. KLC would follow the image as it moved by the window, and with her piecing dark eyes she tried to follow him, only to lose him with another immediate distraction from the crowded street below. She would call him "The Watcher."

As a child, she didn't tell anyone about The Watcher; they wouldn't believe her anyway. "There she goes again. Kizzy making up another story."

None of the women in the house cared much for the men who gathered in the house at night. Over the years they learned how to navigate, stand their ground, and accommodate within limits in order to survive. Kizzy would sit along the stairs in the old brick house and listen to the stories the men would talk about their lives, holding onto the fragile black railing that shook at the first nudge and creaked if your hand was not steady. The steps were wooden and painted white, with cheap black rubber mats on the treads. The staircase was behind a concrete wall between the family's dining room and kitchen. She could smell the pot roast in the oven, the collard greens, corn bread, and sweet potatoes her mom had cooked for the men, and she would listen to their private conversations. Kizzy wondered, *What does that mean? Who were they talking about? When will they do it? Why? How? Can I help?*

The Caldwell house was always filled with people. Emily loved to read, write, and sing. Brownie enjoying talking with the men about work, church, women, politics, and baseball. The Caldwell family was a big one. Brownie Caldwell had four brothers and three sisters who lived in Harrisburg and Emily Harrison Caldwell had three brothers and three sisters who lived in town. The families were very close. Often the families, church friends, and cousins would fill the large old house in the middle of the block. Kizzy lived in the house with her five siblings, parents, two uncles, and a woman from the church whose parents had recently died. The families were all from Georgia. Both the Harrison and Caldwell kids went to school together when they lived down South, but now the Georgia parts of the families were distant. The Harrisons were high yellow (light skin) blacks and the Caldwells were darker-skinned black people. The Caldwells were well liked, more aggressive, and community leaders. The Harrisons were more stand-offish, private people, and better educated. Those were the people Emily and Brownie came from.

In 1938, the Caldwells moved to Pennsylvania. Brownie and Emily married young and moved north where Brownie's older brother and Emily's brother had moved after taking jobs with the railroad. Other relatives had moved north too, mostly settling on the east coast—Philadelphia, New York, and Washington DC, though several ended up in Detroit— mostly working in the auto and steel industries. These were hard-working, blue-collar families who worked to own their homes and provide a better life for their children.

The summer evenings were filled with action. The streets were the entertainment. Television didn't arrive at the home until around 1951 when Kizzy was six years old. The old Philo TV sat in the front room right by the window so everyone who passed by would know the Caldwells had a TV. Kizzy would sit in that window upstairs above the front room while listening and watching as neighbors walked by to look in the front window to see the TV shows. Kizzy's view from the window was her own story book. The view was definitely a live reality show with new and old characters every night. Kizzy could not get enough of it.

Kizzy had just finished eating dinner when she went upstairs to sit on the window ledge. As she ran up the stairs, she heard a rapid banging sound at the front steps. The rest of the family and friends were in the kitchen and with the combination of loud talking and baseball game on the radio, no one else heard the knocking.

Kizzy was halfway up the stairs when she realized no one was coming to open the door. She turned quick to do back down the steps and as she turned, she missed a few steps and fell down the rest of the old, wooden steps. The sound of her falling made such an unusual noise that the conversation in the kitchen came to immediate stop. Everyone ran to the front of the house to see what had happened. At the bottom of the steps near the front door lay Kizzy with tears running down her face. She tried to explain how she fell down the steps and that someone was at the door. Brownie Caldwell checked the door with the other men. Uncle Frank was there with his gun (just in case) because he didn't trust anybody. Most people were afraid of him. He wasn't crazy, but he was a mean soul.

No one was at the door. Kizzy was okay. Her mom put ice on her leg, gave her half an aspirin, and told Kizzy to stop running up and down the steps. "You are going to break your neck one of these days!" Kizzy knew no one believed she heard a knock at the door. They never believed her. Even when she told them how Old Pal had eaten Miss Sally. The poor lady had been missing for eight months, but no one believed Kizzy. People were beginning to blame Miss Sally's boyfriend for her disappearance.

The same night Kizzy heard the knock at the front door, there was a series of shootings in the neighborhood. Kiz would overhear the men talking in the kitchen about other strange things happening in the neighborhood. Luckily, no one was hurt. At that moment, gun shots were heard. The sound was coming from Calder Street. Kizzy heard the men in the kitchen getting up.

She heard her dad say he was going out to see what was going on. Her mom yelled "Brownie, don't leave this house, god dammit! You are always walking into trouble!" Going with Brownie were Uncle Frank and Henry, Cousin Smithy, Rev. Dinkins, and other men from church.

Brownie called out, "Don't worry Emily, nobody's going to get in trouble. We'll be back. We're just gonna run up to the church to make sure everything is okay and then run over to Smithy, Frank, Henry, and Rev. Dinkins' houses. Keep the door locked and the kids upstairs in their room." The men left the house. What happened that night would change these men's lives forever and for everyone.

Chapter 3

Refuge: The Church

R ev. Richard Dinkins was a tall, dark man with a pleasant face and a gentle approach. His clear, distinctive voice was commanding, and when he spoke, he appeared to be looking directly at you. Rev. Dinkins and his wife Marylee were from New York. The talk in town was that they had run a speakeasy and whore house in Brooklyn, New York.

In 1939, Richard Dinkins met Brownie Caldwell at a speakeasy in Brooklyn. Brownie worked for the railroad and visited the speakeasy one night with other men who were traveling through New York with Brownie during a work night off.

Richard met Brownie at the gambling table the night he came into the speakeasy. The two men immediately hit it off. Brownie shared with Richard his life in Harrisburg and Richard talked about giving up his street life and building a church. At the end of the night the two men agreed to stay in touch.

A year later, Richard looked Brownie up and shared his plans again about the church. Brownie got Richard a job at the steel mill and the men remained friends for the rest of their lives. Brownie had a young family too and he decided the idea about building a church with someone was perfect. The same night these men signed the rental lease for the church space they were involved in a terrible car accident in which sixteen people were killed. The cause of the accident was never determined. Both Richard Dinkins and Brownie Caldwell escaped the accident with no visible injuries. Both men were knocked unconscious, and when they awoke in the hospital at nearly the same time in separate rooms, they both told the same story about how the accident happened and what they experienced afterwards.

The men's stories scared little KLC when told to her years later. She believed she saw the accident in her dreams and knew the truth.

Have you ever been prayed for? Has someone laid their hands on you? Or, has anyone every told you what God's plan was for your life? Has anyone ever called you a sinner to your face because you didn't believe what they believed? If not, then you probably never attended a strict Pentecostal church. In the church, women were instructed not to wear pants, shorts, or dresses with arms showing, and married women were rarely seen alone with men other than their husbands or a relative. The preacher was the center of attention. The men in the church supported him. The women in the church either idolized or distrusted the preacher. There was always gossip about adulterous relationships.

The Bible was considered by some an instrument to keep the flock under control. And the values of the church did not apply to all. Passages read out loud were intended to make people feel guilty and reward those who followed the preferences of the pastor and men in the church. At least this is what Kizzy would hear from the "sinners" who she talked with every day after school. Those were Rev. Dinkins' sinners, and she guessed they were her dad's too.

KLC loved the church; the singing, the preaching, the praying, the sprit moving, and touch of hands-on people. She always felt a special bonding with the words the adults would read out loud. She was happy there was a reader of the Bible other than Rev. Dinkins because sometimes he didn't repeat exactly what was read out loud. KLC had her own Bible that Uncle Frank had given her in one of his mean rages, so she could follow along with the church reader. She was too young to truly understand exactly what the words meant, but she took every word literally, exactly as the reader read it, and was confused often by Rev. Dinkins' interpretations. But Kizzy loved to turn the script in her own story and in her own imaginary way she would recite the Ten Commandments in her own terms.

Emily loved watching Kizzy perform and use her imagination. She had been told by a fortune teller when Kizzy was a baby in in her womb how gifted and special she would be. When Emily was eight and a half months pregnant, she was told to let Kizzy go. The child would be hunted her entire life. She would know disappointment, sorrow, and grief, but these events would make her strong and she would be blessed beyond human imagination and God's grace would be with her as she encountered haters, greedy seekers, and others who would betray her. Emily was told she would not be around to help her daughter. But Emily could give her daughter the second most important gift any parent could give a child—besides birth, giving her life—she could leave behind written words of wisdom to guide her daughter. Emily was instructed to continue to write in the notebook she kept under the floorboard. Emily made that commitment.

"Mommy, do you want to hear me say the Ten Commandments?" Kizzy asked.

"Okay Kizzy, go ahead but you got to say the words exactly like you learned them in Sunday school," Emily said.

"Oh mom, I don't want to say it that way. Those words are so boring. Please can I say it my way? My friend the Watcher told me it's okay to say it my way," Kizzy said.

Somewhat amused, Emily pulled up a chair and sat down, then said, "Let me hear your version, Kizzy."

"Thank you so much," Kizzy said. She stood in front of her mom and began.

"Now Moses you are my chosen one. I want you deliver these words to my people. Let them know there is no one else they should worship, no other gods but me.

"You shall not make for yourself an idol in the form of anything.

"You shall not misuse the name of the Lord your God.

"Remember the Sabbath day by keeping it holy.

"Honor your father and your mother.

"You shall not murder.

"You shall not commit adultery.

"You shall not steal.

"You shall not give false testimony against your neighbor.

"You shall not covet your neighbor's house, wife, or property."

KLC looked at her mom and said, "Mom do not let your hearts be troubled. You believe in God; believe also in me. My Father's house has many rooms; if that were not so, would I have told you that I am going there to prepare a place for you? And if I go and prepare a place for you, I will come back and take you to be with me that you also may be where I am. You know the way to the place where I am going."

Emily was in tears. She knew her child was given this message from a higher power.

In Kizzy's darkest moments, these passages would always come to mind to comfort and guide her. Even though she was a child, she was a deep believer. She committed her life to Christ during the summer of 1952 at seven years old. Kizzy was also the adult child in the church, envied by the other young kids and admired at the same time. The adults in the church watched her closely. She was mature beyond her age. For some of the folks in the church she was a peculiar child, a bit too "grown" for their taste. Others considered Kizzy extremely smart and gifted and foresaw the possibilities of her fulfilling all of their hopes, desires, and wishes. The ladies from the church formed a secret group to pray for Kizzy, and each of them prayed for the girl named Kiz

Lamise Caldwell their entire life. Prayers and hopes for a good life. Somehow, these women knew KLC would need those prayers and a praying circle of people to help protect her as she grew up.

Kiz learned about the praying circle late one night while listening to her mom and several women cooking Sunday dinner.

"Emily, let's pray," said a soft unrecognizable voice from the kitchen.

Kiz sat on the step on the staircase along the back wall adjacent to the kitchen and listened to the women praying for her. *Why do I need protection and who is my enemy?* As she wrapped her arms tightly around her legs and rocked back and forth on the steps. She kept asking herself, *Why do I need protection?*

Kizzy was too young then to understand they were praying, asking for God to watch over her because Emily Caldwell had asked the women from the church to keep her daughter in prayer. Marylee Dinkins helped lead the payer.

On Wednesday nights, the women would meet at the church. The wood-planked floors, with folded chairs, an old house with walls taken down to make room for the worshipers, larger windows draped with cheap deep red velvet curtains, and praying cloths, Bibles throughout the rooms, a large picture of Jesus on the front wall facing the members, and pictures of the last supper and Bible verses throughout the worship area. The men who worked on the church built a riser in front so Rev. Dinkins would be elevated up whenever

he addressed the congregation. A large table was placed
between Rev. Dinkins and the founding members sat off
to the side in the front. These were the deacons. These were
working class men who found power in the church and with
their religion.

Every Wednesday, Friday, and Sunday morning and evening there was church. Young KLC would attend all the services but leave early because of school the next day or because
it was just too late. She listened deeply as a young child to
the messages about heaven and hell and she vowed to live by
the teachings even though she didn't understand them. She
always felt God was trying to tell her something and definitely watching over her.

Dreams

Colin reminded KLC to bring a sweater, a copy of the
National Geographic, a knife, and the tape. The girls had
plans about their life and Harrisburg was not a part of it.
The girls decided to run far away. They would leave when
Colin's dad was out of town. Colin would steal her dad's
car during his next trip out of town. She would take the car
while her mom was asleep from too much alcohol and her
sister and brother were away. KLC would take the church
money (her dad was the church treasurer) and he always
went to the bank on Mondays, so they had to take the money
on Sunday night. The collection would be much larger as it
would include the collections from the week. The girls were
thirteen and fourteen years old. They would meet on Front
Street near State at 11:00 pm on the third Sunday of the

month. Both girls could easily slip away. Colin would pack the gun. The gun was in a closet in a Rankin department store shoe box.

She could breathe, finally calming down. How far had she run with the tears still flowing from her eyes and the ghosts of her childhood still haunting her? As she flipped the pages of the magazine, she stared at so many unknown places and people, wondering when she would escape this prison she was locked inside. Why didn't she learn to swim when she had a chance? A question she asked herself many times. There they stood all around, particularly two of them were watching her again. She would take a quick nap before deciding what to do next. "KLC, KLC, KLC, wake-up!" She heard the voice urging her. She couldn't move. Was she dreaming or was this real? "Yes, Colin, I'm trying to sleep."

Colin Rankin was KLC's childhood friend. They were best friends from third grade through twelfth grade. After their high school graduation, they parted ways never to see each again. Many years later KLC met a young woman on a plane name Carla who was returning from her mother's funeral and needing to talk and have someone listen to her. Carla shared a lot about herself and told Kiz an amazing story about betrayal and the secrets and lies her mother kept and what she left behind. Carla was on her way back home to France where she lived and practiced as a lawyer. She was a biracial child with a lovely French accent. Yet, there was something very familiar about her. KLC could not put her finger on it. She told KLC her mom wrote a letter to someone but never addressed the envelope. She only had the letters of the person on the front of the envelope.

The young woman Carla started to cry. She then said. "My mother would want me to find KLC." Carla apologized for talking too much. She took a small pill from her purse, sipped some water, and fell asleep. Kiz sat there in silence and thought about Colin. The two women did not speak again until the plan landed in Paris. They said goodbye and went their separate ways.

Being the first wasn't easy. There were always high expectations; she was always on, always visible, yet KLC felt invisible when it counted the most. KCL entered the court room as they all stood. She knew this would be the end of her career as a judge. She never felt justice was being served and until she solved what happened in her hometown and what she saw that night on the windowsill, she would never be free to pursue her purpose. She had dreamed of becoming a Supreme Court judge since she was a child. After her senate campaign and years as a prosecutor and college professor, she decided to accept the judgeship. It was truly an honor, but it was not her calling. There was something else eating at her.

Who the hell were Clay and Mason? When they approached her about the resignation, she had just submitted she realized she had made the right decision. KLC was always a first, and she understood that was her destiny. However, what concerned her most was the fact that the only chair in the room with a woman in it was the one she sat in. All those years as she fought her way to the top, was she not conscious or aware she was the only woman one in the room? Didn't she think mentoring more women to step into her roles was the right thing to do?

Kiz was still haunted by her childhood. The murders, the kidnapping, and bombings were unsolved work she still needed to solve. After Kiz resigned from the judgeship, she decided to solve these cases independently. She would first take some time off and spend more time with her husband and her lover. She loved them both but needed to make a choice. Maybe what she needed was three months in France to help clear her head, perhaps do some writing or something like that. Kiz remembered the young woman on the plane. Carla was her name. Maybe she would try to find her the next time she was in Paris.

She wrote in her diary:

Dear Watcher,

I finally understand why you left me. I never truly got over you and when I realized who you were… Well let's say, you were gone to never appear again.

You were the man in my dreams, the watcher, the protector, and the chill in the night and the warmth in the morning, the whisper in the dark. My lover, protector, challenger and adversary. You were all of that and more. Did we first meet that night in the green fields at the old farmhouse when I was seven years old? Was it there when you held my hand for the first time and changed my life?

When they found me, I was wrapped in a blanket in the middle of farm country.

No one knew then how I got there or how I survived for a whole week without a trace. It was you, the Watcher. You were there then and through most of my life as my guide, some would say my angel. When I had to let you go, my life changed. I changed. I guess I didn't need your guidance anymore. Perhaps it's my turn to hold someone's hand, to become their watcher.

Kiz had spent her entire life for this moment, landing on solid ground with a strong sense of purpose and determination.

"Mrs. Caldwell," someone called as the people were returning from the lunch break. "Are you ready?" KLC returned to the stage to continue telling Kiz's story.

The Incident at School – Monday, May at 3:30pm

Hamilton Elementary School sat on the middle of the block on 6th street, between Harris and Calder, just three blocks from the Caldwell house. Kizzy was in second grade and Mr. Johnson was her teacher. She did not like him. He was a mean and angry man. She later learned he was a military man and had spent twenty years in the military before becoming a teacher, lost many of his friends during the war but was surrounded by many who admired his boldness, worldliness, and smarts. He was popular at his church, in the choir, a deacon, and chief organizer of events. He was a tall and good-looking man. People called him General Johnson.

Kizzy never knew if that was true or not. Mr. Johnson took an interest in Kizzy from the first day he saw her in the school building. There was something about this child that he felt was very special and would need his protection or guidance. Mr. Johnson made a mental note to protect Kizzy for as long as he could.

"Sorry, Mr. Johnson, I didn't see you standing there," came the voice of the confident girl as she bumped into the teacher who towered over her. She was running down the hall with the other kids at the sound of the 3:30 pm bell which signaled the school day was over.

Kizzy was always in a hurry to get on to the next thing. She also had plans for what was next.

"Stop running, Miss Caldwell," Mr. Johnson said. He always called her Miss Caldwell and lectured her. "Walk with your head high and straighten your back. You'll get out of here soon enough. Ladies don't run, they walk with intention," Mr. Johnson said.

Kizzy slowed down and walked out of the building with a few of the teachers who were leaving the building a bit earlier due to some major event later that afternoon. She couldn't quite understand what they were talking about, but it sounded like they were pretty excited.

Similar to other days, Kizzy started the short walk from school to home on Cumberland Street. She was thinking about Mr. Johnson and why he always called her out like that. It was really embarrassing. Why did he call her Miss Caldwell instead of Kizzy like the other teachers? Kizzy started walking faster, almost about to run when she heard the roaring engine of an approaching car. That's when she saw the blue and white car turning the corner toward the school.

The car was making a particular noise, which she thought was the repeated revving of a car engine. The noise surprised the school kids as they watched the fast-approaching car coming toward them. The car suddenly stopped and all four of the car doors opened at the same time. What Kizzy and others then witnessed, no words can fully describe.

The kids and teachers were in shock as they looked on. Out of the car stepped humanlike figures, each of them on fire and screaming words no one understood except Kizzy and Colin.

The little girls looked at each when they heard the burning figures say, "Run, girls, run! Run, Kizzy! Take care of Colin and run. Run, girls, run!" The figures continued to burn to just ashes.

The blue and white car then disappeared. The crowd stood stunned by what they had just witnessed.

News of the incident near the school on 6th Street spread. No one knew exactly what had happened, but stories where developing. The center of 6th and Hamilton Streets became crowded with older kids from the high school down the street, people from the neighborhood, and cars passing by. The police arrived and were keeping people away from the bodies and trying to keep order at the same time. The black ash corpses laid there in plain sight. As Kizzy stood there and looked from where she had perched herself, she carefully tried to listen for the voices of the black corpses that lay in front of her, their eyes still open. She thought she saw a movement from one of their lips. She started to cry, tears rolling down her cheeks. She lifted up the hem of her favorite yellow and black skirt to swipe her face, then saw something strange on her shoes.

Something awful looking, dark brown and wet. Her eyes followed the brown stuff around her shoes, and she could see a pattern. The brown stuff was coming from the corpses and was all over her shoes and running through the crowd. She lifted her head to glance again at the corpse in front of her. Kizzy could have sworn the corpse looked straight at her and with just its eyes said, "Run Kiz Lamise Caldwell, run!"

KLC moved away from where she stood and weaved her way through the crowd.

"Where are you going?" Colin called out as she tried to catch up with KLC. Colin's older sister from the high school grabbed her little sister's arm and they ran off from the crowd in a different direction.

Kizzy saw Alice and Larry, waving at them to signal she was headed home. On the way Kizzy looked at her shoes again and noticed the brown stuff had mostly disappeared. She looked up and down the street for the dark brown lines.

She could see a brown circle near where the crowd had gathered. She turned around and started skipping her way home both excited and scared, wanting to be the first to tell her mom what had happened. When she heard the familiar sounds from the juke joint and church both starting up at the same time, it was a sign there was not much farther to go before she was home and safe.

When she got home, no one was there.

Kizzy changed from her school clothes to her play clothes and sat in the window for a while, waiting for her mom and siblings to come home. Then she fell asleep on the floor below the window.

The Death of Emily Caldwell – 4:30pm

"Wake up KLC, wake up!" She heard her mother's voice at the same time as her mother was grabbing her arm. "Where are your brothers and sisters?"

Kizzy told her where she last saw them and started to tell her mom about the burning bodies at school.

Emily held her daughter tight. Kizzy was surprised to get a hug, "Mom what's the matter? What's the matter?" Kizzy asked.

Emily looked at Kizzy and kissed her on both cheeks. "Kiz Lamise Caldwell, you are my blessed child and I love you very much."

Before her mother could finish, someone was banging on the front door. Kizzy first thought it was her sisters and brothers, then quickly realized they would not be knocking on the door. Emily stood up. "Kizzy, I'll right back. Be quiet and get under the bed," she whispered as she closed the door.

Kizzy was scared.

Then the sound: *Bang, bang, bang!* The sound was coming from downstairs. Kizzy heard a car engine. She crawled out from under the bed, stood on her tippy toes and peeked out the window. There was the blue and white car in front of the house. Too frightened to move, Kizzy waited for her mom to come back up the steps to get her. From the window, she could see people from the juke joint and candy store walking across the street and gathering in front of 625 Cumberland, some with their hands over their mouths, others crying, a few shouting, but most were just standing beneath the window. She heard Old Pal bark out to her two times, calling her name.

Kizzy wasn't sure what had happened. Slowly she moved toward the door, afraid to open it. When she did, she was relieved to see no one there. She called out for her mother. "Mom, Mom, Mom, are you alright?"

As Kizzy approached the bottom step, she saw the brown soles of the new black flats that were just bought through the Sears catalog, stockings rolled down at the ankle, feet crossed at the ankles, and both feet sticking out of the partially closed front door. Emily Caldwell still had her clothes on from cleaning at the downtown hotels where she worked.

Kizzy knew something awful had happened. She heard the crowd and saw them from her window. Where were her sisters and brothers, and the others who lived in the house?

When Kizzy opened the front door her mother's body rolled to the front edge of the concrete step. The crowd gasped, called her name, asking if she and everyone else was okay? Kizzy just nodded. Realizing her mom was hurt. Blood flowed every which way, reminding Kizzy of the dark stuff that was on her shoes from earlier that afternoon. She bent down to kiss her mother's cheek as her mom took her last breath.

Kizzy's mom had been shot three times. She died on the concrete step with Kizzy by her side. No one witnessed the actual shooting. The police asked Kizzy about the shooting and tried to determine who else was in the house at the time. Kizzy told them no one else was home, just her and her mom.

The police took some notes and asked the child if she had someone to stay with her for the night. Kizzy said her sisters and brother would be home soon, and her dad and uncle would be home from work soon too. At that point one of the neighbors stepped up and said they would watch the child until the rest of the family arrived. The police then told the crowd to leave, nothing else to see, and left the child home by herself after the tragic death of her mother.

Kizzy sat by the window and watched as her mom's body was removed from the step. It felt like hours had passed while she waited for the others to arrive. She was really tired from the emotions of the day and overwhelmed with grief from her mother's death and the events near the school.

Little Kizzy fell asleep on the windowsill, and as she slept visions of the burned corpses remained in her dreams and the visions of her mother's feet crossed at the ankles sticking out of the door flooded her thoughts. When she woke up it was around 6:30 pm. The house was still quiet. The noise outside was different. Occasionally, Kizzy could hear Old Pal bark, the juke joint was a quieter than usual, and she didn't hear anything from the church. Kizzy was really scared and hungry. She was there in the old house with the sinner lady from across the street watching over her. She had to leave the house.

Kizzy decided to go to the church and look for her family. Did she fall asleep and dream everything or did these things really happen? The sinner lady from across the street was asleep when Kizzy tiptoed down the steps. Kizzy could smell the whisky and she saw the glass. Alcohol was not allowed in the Caldwell home, so this was definitely a sinner.

She opened the door and the blood from her mother's body was still on the steps. Kizzy's own hands were crusted with the blood that had spilled over onto her. She didn't get a chance to wash her hands or change her clothes before she fell asleep. So, blood was all over her clothes. Kiz decided not to take the time to change now.

Outside there was a nasty, almost unbearable smell in the air. Kizzy's stomach was churning from both hunger and fatigue. She turned the corner and headed to Calder Street toward the church. The smell was so bad she covered her nose with her bloody shirt. Street closed signs and yellow tape were everywhere. People were walking through the street with masks on, no one cared to notice Kizzy. She spotted Rev. Dinkins' wife Marylee who was her mom's friend. She ran over to Mrs. Dinkins with tears in her eyes.

Marylee Dinkins asked, "Are you okay Kizzy?"

Kizzy did not answer. Instead, the child fell into Mrs. Dinkins arms.

Marylee Dinkins carried the child into the church where many others had gathered, all wearing masks and gloves. Some were praying, others crying, and others sitting and staring into space.

Kizzy struggled to sit up. "Mom is dead, and blood is everywhere on the front steps at home," she said loud enough for others to hear. Mrs. Dinkins rocked the special child with a knowing squeeze. The church was silent.

Kizzy lifted and turned her head to Mrs. Dinkins and in a whisper asked, "Where is my dad? My sisters and brothers? Are they dead too?" Mrs. Dinkins tried to look at the child directly in her eyes, but she couldn't. Marylee Dinkins said, "Nobody knows where anybody is. What we do know is flesh is burning."

Kizzy closed her eyes and slept.

Marylee Dinkins was a big woman, she picked up the child and carried her to the front of the church laying Kizzy down on a well-cushioned bench near the altar and covered her with a purple and gold choir robe to keep her warm.

Marylee Dinkins came to Harrisburg with her husband to start a new life. The church and new friends in the community gave her a chance to be a better person, to give back, and try to live a normal life. Marylee couldn't be happier with how everything thing had turned out since moving to Harrisburg. The church had grown from thirty members to over 1,200 and she was well known and respected in the community. It wasn't enough. She wanted power, real power, and only Kiz Lamise Caldwell could make that happen.

Chapter 4

The Kidnapping

Harrisburg, Pennsylvania. Monday, May 5, 1952
(Early Evening)

M arylee walked toward her private office which was hidden from public view and impossible to find unless you were familiar with the church layout or had been invited there by her. She was worried about the plan and wondered whether or not it had been executed as instructed. Time was running out for her and the others, and the only way out was through Kizzy. She had to act fast and then get back to the child she left sleeping on the front pew before the others arrived and took the child away.

When Marylee approached the door to her office, she could see a glow of a purple and gold light shining from under her door.

She turned the knob and opened the door. Three men were positioned at different locations inside her office. They were waiting for her.

Fearless and power hungry as she was, nothing frightened her more than being so close to her dreams and losing everything. Marylee had already lost her soul.

Marylee had forgotten to lock the door from earlier in the day.

The door was open.

"Come in. Close the door. Sit down Marylee. We're here to collect the girl. Where is she?" a familiar voice said.

Marylee sat down. She knew the men and thought she could probably buy some more time and reason with them. She needed more time to train the child in the ways of the other world and how to use her special gifts to gain power over others.

Marylee had no luck with the men as they were on strict orders. There was no reasoning because the men were on a mission to bring Kiz Lamise Caldwell to Shadow Corporation's recovery center within the next twelve hours. The men explained to Marylee that time had run out because Shadow Corporation had received information that Landing Enterprise had located the girl and were planning a kidnapping within the next twenty-four hours.

Marylee was surprised by the news. She had no idea Landing Enterprise was this close to knowing Kizzy's identity. She agreed to bring Kizzy to the agreed upon meeting place before the deadline. The men trusted Marylee and accepted the agreement that Marylee would bring the girl herself to the others later that night.

Marylee walked the men out of a back exit that led to a dark and narrow alley. Marylee and the men wanted to avoid being seen by the people who had gathered inside and outside of the church.

Marylee walked back to the sanctuary where she had left Kizzy. Fortunately, the pew was covered as she had left it, and the bundle was still there. Marylee was confident Kizzy was still asleep and exhausted from all that she had experienced in one day. Marylee thought she would first clean Kizzy up before taking her to the recovery center, and later others would take her to Shadow's special place for her to stay.

Unfortunately, the church was full of people seeking refuge from the awfulness of the odor coming from the burning flesh outside and growing unrest in the city.

Marylee could hear the people inside the church chattering about the events of the day; the incident at the school earlier and later the murder of Emily Caldwell. She overheard a few people asking about the Caldwell's little girl Kizzy and wondering how she had escaped the tragedy at school and the murder of her mom. People were whispering amongst themselves about the police and questioning whether the police and mayor's office had done enough to protect little Kizzy and the rest of family.

Two women came into the church, their faces and head were covered, they wore long black shirts and short double-breasted, fitted, high-collar jackets trimmed in gold at the cuffs, gold buttons, and stripes and stars on their sleeves, signifying some sort of rank in the military.

The women kneeled at the altar while Marylee continued negotiations with the men from Shadow Corporation.

Kizzy was asleep on the bench in front of them wrapped in the colors of "glory" as the Watcher had told them she would be. The women walked over to the pew, one gently poking the girl with an injection of a mild sedative to help her sleep longer. The heavier of the two women, Eula, lifted Kizzy from the robe while the other emptied the contents of the black plastic bag she carried into the church under the robe on the cushioned church pew. The women exited out of the back side door of the church right a few feet behind the altar to a door that led to sinner's alley and a waiting car. No one saw them leave the church or notice the exchange that took place.

Marylee sat next to the bundle in front of her and softly spoke, "Wake up Kizzy. Kizzy, wake up."

She slowly uncovered the purple and gold choir robe from the top of the body. There was no movement. Marylee thought she would first clean up the little girl and get her something to eat. The little girl really needed a bath. The odor was almost unbearable. When the covering fell off, what was revealed to Marylee and the others who had gathered at the front of the church was the horrible site of a dead animal, a dog or cat with its eyes wide open. There was an immediate hush from those who witnessed the discovery with Marylee. Only she knew that the girl Kizzy was wrapped in the choir robe and placed on that pew. There was near panic in the church as news of the dead animal began to spread and word that Marylee called out for Kizzy's name as she unwrapped the robe that was on the front pew.

Kizzy was seven years old when she disappeared from the church on Calder Street, the same day she had witnessed the burning corpses at school and her mother's death.

The women knew they had to clean up the little girl before taking her to the landing boat. Clothes were selected for her, and she would be bathed in the Susquehanna River and rubbed down in exotic oils from far away. Kizzy's clothes were burned and replaced with a plain white sweater and black pants. They placed her inside a blue 1952 Ford panel truck where a small carton of milk, a peanut butter and jelly sandwich, and apple were placed where the girl could find the food later. The women had used the truck before to track and capture others who were released from Landing Enterprise. Specifically for the kidnap from the church, she was wrapped in a gold and purple blanket and placed in a cage and would remain sedated throughout the cleaning process. She was dressed in purple and wrapped up before they got her to Landing's Boat.

Kizzy was hot, thirsty, and hungry. Her movements were constrained she felt the wire tiny holes small enough for her figures to enter; she was inside of something small. She was confused and scared. She felt as if she was locked inside of a cage on a roller coaster ride. It was dark; she could hear the sound of rapid tapping around her and could feel the impact of rhythmic crushing of something she couldn't identify.

"Hello?" Kizzy cried out, "Anybody there? Hello, I'm here! Help me, help me!" She was crying so hard that the ladies in the truck turned the music up real loud to drown out the crying girl's voice. Kizzy could hear the song. "Am I dead too?"

Where was she? Was she dreaming? Had she died too? Was this hell? She couldn't see anything, but she could barely hear the voices of women talking about getting to a place called the Landing before sunrise. The voices were low, unfamiliar, and infrequent. What she did hear them say was the package had to be delivered by sunrise and handled very carefully.

The sedative still had some effect. Kiz began to fall asleep when suddenly her small body shifted forward against the wiry mess that surrounded her. The music and rapid tapping sound had both stopped. She barely heard the voices of others talking. There was clapping, then silence.

She felt responsible for everything that happened that day. Kizzy closed her eyes and began to pray. "God, I am so sorry for what happened today. I didn't know who to tell. They never believe me. They say I make things up. Please God, don't send me to hell. I am so sorry and promise I will tell the truth and not let anyone else get hurt."

Tuesday, morning May 6

The sun was rising as the back of the truck was opened and Kizzy opened her eyes. She was overwhelmed with mixed emotions, realizing she was in a car and wire animal kennel but none of that mattered much as the sun appearing right in front of her. She smiled knowing she was not in hell, but wondered where she was. She was no longer afraid. There were people all around the truck and standing close to the sun. She couldn't see their faces, only hear the sounds of their voices and then someone draped in gold and purple approached the truck and lifted the cage out and appeared to extend a hand to help her out of the cage. Kizzy reached for the hand, but nothing was there as she stepped on the gravel road.

The people and the car who were there a second ago were all gone. She looked around and it was only her standing on the gravel road. She didn't know what to do. So, she did what she always did when she faced a dilemma: she ran.

She could see the river straight ahead and something big, like a pyramid, gold and shiny, sitting in the middle of river. Kizzy could not stop running. She finally collapsed from fatigue and excitement at the edge of the river when the two women who had kidnapped her from the church helped her stand up and began to guide her along the edge of the river. Kizzy was not scared. She didn't think she was dead or in hell or heaven.

Finally, the women spoke, "I am Eula, and my job is to take you to the Landing Boat."

"And I am Iva. My job is to help take care of you until we reach the Boat's transport point.

Kizzy had never heard anyone talk as fast as the women were speaking and she couldn't quite understand everything they were saying to her. She asked what's a transport point and landing and what was that thing in the river?

Again, Eula spoke first. "You have already seen Landing's Boat. It's over there in the river. It won't be there much longer. We are taking you there.

"Please can we stop for a minute? My knee hurts and I have to pee."

"Go behind the rock and pee," Iva said.

After Kizzy returned, Iva looked at Kizzy's knee.

"Your knee is okay," Iva said as she pulled out a small bag and handed it to Kizzy. Inside was a peanut butter and jelly sandwich.

"How will we get to the middle of the river? I can't swim," Kizzy asked Eula.

"The Boat will come to us," Eula said as she looked at Kizzy's puzzled facial expression.

"I don't understand. How?" Kizzy asked.

"Landing's Boat will move closer to meet us at a special place. We will be there soon," Iva said in a much softer tone.

Eula and Iva were both in their early thirties, born and raised in Rabat, Morocco during a time of French control. They were identified in their teens as soldiers for Landing

Enterprise because of their toughness, independence, and a recognition in their hometown for an ability to see the future. Both women tried to ignore their gift for seeing into the future, but as they grew older their involvement in underground clandestine activities grew and their reputation throughout Morocco during the war made them highly sought after by various underground groups.

Landing Enterprise saw them as a perfect match to help execute their plan to gather the most gifted individuals in the world to sell future predictions to massive and growing underground and legitimate markets. Landing Enterprise sought individuals who were intellectually brilliant and those who had extraordinary psychic powers. Landing's plan had been to combine the two abilities to become the world's most powerful source of information.

Eula and Iva still used their abilities but for different reasons. This was their first trip to this part of the world and the first time with a child. They never asked questions, just focused on the traveler and made sure the traveler was prepared to enter the opening of the Landing Transfer Boat. Neither woman had ever seen anyone return once they entered the Landing space.

"We need to get the girl ready now," Iva said to Eula.

Kizzy looked at the women, wondering what they meant.

Eula said, "We can't waste any time. Did you bring the tools?"

Iva responded, "Yes, in my bag. Should we cut or shave the hair?"

"Shaving will be quicker."

"Are you going to shave off all of my hair?" Kizzy asked.

"Yes," replied Iva.

"I don't want my hair shaved," said Kizzy.

"You must do what we say," said Eula in a sterner voice.

"No! I will not shave my hair," Kizzy insisted.

"Please take off your clothes. You will wear the clothing in this bag," Iva said as she handed a bag to Kizzy. Iva then turned to prepare the shaving mix.

As Kizzy was putting on the long-sleeved, black high-collar dress with gold trim and black slippers, Iva noticed Kizzy was shivering. There was something else the women noticed about this traveler that was different. Eula noticed it too.

Kizzy screamed out, "I WANT TO GO HOME. Please, please. Please can you take me back? I don't want to go to that thing, it's not safe." Then Kizzy started to cry.

Eula could see the boat slowly approaching and figuring it would be another thirty minutes.

"We must hurry and finish up. Iva needs to shave your head," Eula stated.

Kizzy replied, "But, I don't want to go, I don't want my head shaved, I want to go home."

Eula positioned herself closer to the girl who had perched herself on a large boulder and was crying uncontrollably. Iva stood there next to Kizzy and both women knew the child would not be ready to enter the Landing.

Kizzy kept crying and repeating, "Take me home, I want to go home!"

Eula and Iva walked a few feet away from Kizzy to talk in private. The women could feel the wind and see the waves of the river flowing more rapidly indicating a boat or vessel of some sort was in the water.

"What should we do? We can't force her to board the Boat," Iva said. "We need to help her, Iva. The girl is not ready to join Landing Enterprise," Eula stated.

The two women did something they had never done before. They walked back to Kizzy, who was now wiping her nose on the black dress and looking at the women who stood on each side of her.

Instinctively, Kizzy reached out to hold Eula's and Iva's hands. The women looked into Kizzy's eyes for a few seconds.

Then Eula announced, "We have a plan."

Eula, Iva, and Kizzy starting walking back to the truck. Iva placed a beautifully woven purple and gold blanket around Kizzy shoulders. As they walked back to the truck the women tried to talk to the young girl about what happening. They also tried to explain the kidnapping. They knew she was much too young to understand, but hopefully one day it would all make sense.

Kizzy was thinking about what the women were sharing with her. Kizzy still did not fully understand. She asked, "Ms. Eula and Ms. Iva, when you took me out of the truck, I saw a bright gold and purple light over the river and there were people singing and I think shadows standing all around me. Was that real or was I dreaming?" Kizzy asked.

The women looked at each other.

Iva spoked first. "Kizzy, what's real for you will not always be real for others. You are a very special girl and it's okay to see things that others do not see. You have a gift that others do not." Eula added, "We did not see what you saw. It was me who lifted you out of the truck. What we saw was the sun rise. You, me, and Iva have been alone the entire time." "But I saw them, the light, and he tried to take my hand! I felt safe then," Kizzy pleaded.

The women sighed. Eula continued, "You may have seen angels and felt surrounded by their protection because you were open to receiving a special anointment. You may have been blessed today."

Kizzy asked, "Where are the angels now?"

The women smiled and Iva responded, "Your guardian angels never leave your side. They are all around you. Most of the time you can't see them, but they are there."

Kizzy was listening carefully, as she tried hard to understand what Eula and Iva were trying to tell her.

The three of them walked in silence for a long time.

Suddenly Kizzy asked, "Are you angels or sinners?"

The women were surprised by the question.

Laughing out loud they reached for Kizzy's hand as they walked toward their waiting truck straight ahead.

As Eula and Iva opened the passenger doors they turned to Kizzy and Iva said, "We are both angels and sinners."

The little girl jumped into the back seat of the truck wide-eyed and anxious to go home and talk more about angels and sinners.

The Landing Boat never arrived and was no longer in the river. They were already warned the women were captivated by the girl and their own truths.

Eula and Iva's work with the Landing was done and they both would move on to new adventures. To lose a traveler was not something either of them had experienced before. But there was something about Kizzy that caused them to put her desires first. She was too young to be ready to make a big decision that would change her life.

Iva and Eula decided to face the consequences, although they were told by previous soldiers that losing a recruit happens sometimes. To force a gifted one aboard was not a part of the Landing's approach. The organization learned many years ago that the loss of psychic powers and other gifts was often directly related to forced compliance. Still, agents and soldiers were usually dismissed after losing a recruit.

Kiz Caldwell was identified by dark traffickers in future prediction as exceptionally gifted. She was identified at birth and almost kidnapped by a nurse who worked underground for a competing organization, Shadow Corporation, and a friend of Marylee Landrieu Dinkins.

The doctor who intervened to save the girl from the earlier kidnapping attempt worked as a consultant for Landing Enterprise leading the research into gene typing and traits of psychic and gifted babies. His name was Dr. Kline, who happened to be the doctor who delivered Kizzy in 1945. He promised himself to keep an eye on the girl to confirm his suspicions of her abilities and destiny as one of seven people in the world with a particular power. Science and technology had not advanced as aggressively as Dr. Kline's research; but it would be just a matter of time before the theory and practice would intersect.

Dr. Kline was the primary contact for Eula and Iva and Landings' primary person in Harrisburg related to the girl. Dr. Kline was notified that the mission to bring Kiz Lamise Caldwell into the organization was aborted due to the child's resistance.

Chapter 5

Grief

B rownie was out of town on Monday and Tuesday of that week. He had accepted extra work on a new rail line in upstate New York for three to four days. When these opportunities came most of the men took the opportunity. Plus, Brownie was saving up to buy a new house for Emily and the kids. He wanted to get them out of the 8th ward and give them a chance to see a different side of life.

Emily agreed he should take the extra work. She realized that he would not be able to call everyday but would check in as much as he could. Finding a pay phone in the areas where the men were working was not always easy. On Wednesday morning, Brownie found a phone and tried calling Emily. He didn't get an answer. He kept calling whenever he got a break. Brownie was getting concerned. He had overheard some of the men talking about some trouble down in Harrisburg. After three different tries, he finally called Emily's sister Kara to make sure everything was okay.

"Hello Kara, Brownie here calling from work in New York. Hey listen, I've been trying to reach Emily and the kids and no one is answering? Is everybody okay?" Brownie asked.

Kara took a deep breath. Then she began, "Brownie, we've tried to reach you. I just got your number this morning from the union rep."

"Why, what's going on?" Brownie asked.

Kara continued: "Emily is dead, Brownie. She was murdered Monday afternoon; the police don't know who did it. Kizzy was the only one home at the time. The police left Kizzy with your neighbor Mildred." Kara paused. "Mildred fell asleep, and when she woke-up, Kizzy was gone. No one has seen Kizzy since. Your other girls are with me, and the boys are with their uncle Smithy."

Brownie was numb. He couldn't find the words to react. His heart was beating fast against what felt like a stone wall inside of him. He thought he would explode any minute.

Kara waited a moment, the silence on the other end brought more tears to her eyes ... she too was overwhelmed with the grief that had struck the family and the city.

Brownie's voice was hardly recognizable when he spoke. "Kara, I will be home tonight – tell the kids I'm on the way." Then he hung up.

Kara sobbed quietly as she placed the phone on the receiver.

Thursday, May 8, 1952: Harrisburg, Pennsylvania (Morning)

The city needed to move forward from the unusual activities in certain parts of town, particularly the 8th ward. There was the school incident, and then a gas leak that sent scores of people to the local hospital and sent large numbers of residents from the 8th ward to evacuation shelters.

Families had involuntarily split up. Many families had limited knowledge of where other members of their family were sent. A few houses had exploded near the railroad tracks, and it was believed many lives were lost. The town had very little time to mourn or identify the four men whose corpses were thrown from the blue and white car on Monday. People were scared and parents would not let their kids go back to school even though the news reports said it was safe to do so.

Yet, parts of town were noisy with the sounds of music blasting from the bars, and dogs were barking and roaming the street in packs. TVs and radios were turned up extra high as people tried to capture every bit of news possible while others were trying to block out all memory of what had occurred during the week. Most people just wanted things back to normal.

Police patrolled the neighborhoods. Strange cars were seen throughout the city's 8th ward. Gawkers and reporters were talking to everyone they could about the Caldwell girl's kidnapping, the death of Emily Caldwell, the family, where was the father, the corpses, the missing people, and the strange smell of burning flesh. News outlets were taking pictures and asking random people impersonal questions about their experience and loss.

Kizzy Caldwell's disappearance wasn't a high priority for anyone outside of her family and a few others in the city. Yet, questions about her being missing were being asked. Marylee knew she was missing before anyone else. Later, the girl's disappearance would become a major local story.

"What the hell happened?" a frustrated, angry, and grieving Brownie Caldwell asked of Marylee and Rev. Dinkins as they sat at the kitchen table in the Caldwell home on Cumberland Street.

"Why Emily? Why? Who would want to kill Emily? And, my little Kizzy, where is she? Nothing is making any sense. Emily and Kizzy? Who would do this? I should have been here to protect my family. I promise to make whoever did this to Emily and took Kizzy pay. I promise I will." Brownie said.

Rev. Dinkins interrupted, "Brownie, man I know you are hurting and wish you were here to protect your Emily. But man, you were doing what you had to do, working, trying to make a living for your family, being a railroad man with the long hours and days away so your family can live in this house you provided for them. We'll find Kizzy. Marylee last saw her at the church on Monday night. I'll tell you more about that later. For now, let's finalize the funeral arrangements for Emily's funeral." Brownie turned to look at Marylee, who had an uneasy expression on her face as she sipped the soda she held in her hands.

"Do you know where we can find Kizzy?" Brownie asked with a glimmer of hope.

"No. She was alive and at the church Monday night. Someone took her from there. They left a dead animal on the pew where she had been sleeping," Marylee said.

Brownie bowed and shook his head.

Rev. Dinkins stood up and motioned for Marylee to do the same. He placed his hands on Brownie's shoulder and tapped them twice. Brownie tried to stand. But Richard motioned for him to remain seated.

"Hey man I'm going to take Marylee home, give you some time with your kids. I'll get back to you later and then we'll finish up the funeral arrangements for Emily."

When Brownie looked up to acknowledge his words, Richard could see the grief on his friend's face.

The Dinkins' walked out of the kitchen. The five other Caldwell children were on the steps and in the living room, listening to every word. The children did not say anything. Richard reached over Marylee to give each of the kids a hug and to say how very sorry he was. He also reassured them that they would find Kizzy. Rev. Dinkins then asked the kids to join him as he prayed for the family and the safe return of Kizzy. Marylee did not join the family in prayer.

During the week the kids' lives had been disrupted too. The Caldwell kids spent time between the school shelter and relatives who lived close by. The older children took take care of the younger ones after they returned home waiting for their father to return from work in New York.

Richard Dinkins drove both himself and Marylee the few blocks to the church, parking in his reserved space in front of the church. The ride from the Caldwell's had been tense, short and quiet. After he parked, he reached over and pulled Marylee's arm to prevent her from opening the door and getting out of the car.

"What was Kizzy doing at the church on Monday night and where were you?" Richard Dinkins asked.

Marylee struggled to remove her arm from his tight grip. In an angry, determined gesture, she leaned over and bit Richard Dinkins on the forearm. "Let me go!" Marylee screamed as her teeth landed on his forearm and about to go deeper as Richard immediately let her go while calling out to her.

"Marylee, what have you done with the little girl."

Marylee did not respond. She opened the door to get out and closed the door without emotion as she headed toward the church, with the intentions of locking herself inside her office and destroying any evidence of her affiliation with the Shadow Organization.

When Rev. Dinkins reached the church, he got out of the car, locked the car and walked up the steep steps into the church. The time had finally come for him to confront Marylee about the documents he had found hidden under the floor panel of their whorehouse in New York. He wanted to believe she had changed and had given up the old ways of her evil mother and grandmother. Witchcraft and voodoo had been a practice in Marylee's family for generations. He read the document. She had signed a pledge to sell her soul to the Shadow Corporation in exchange for the ultimate power to rule over the section of the organization that influenced how people thought about their future. She was told the organization was in competition for newborn babies and children four to nine who had been identified as having extraordinary psychic ability. The name Caldwell was on the list. The only problem was Marylee didn't have the extraordinary abilities that her mother, grandmother or great grandmother had.

Rev. Dinkins kept what he knew to himself. When they moved to Harrisburg in 1939, the relationship with Brownie Caldwell developed into a brotherhood and the families became close. Also, the two men had developed an almost scared bond after their accident on Front Street in Harrisburg. He almost forgot that Marylee was the one who urged him to seek out Brownie and move to Harrisburg. She too had met Brownie that night at their brothel in New York. Rev. Dinkins now wondered if Brownie showing up at that night was a coincidence or if the meeting between the two men had been a set-up.

Richard knocked hard on the locked office door. "Open the door Marylee, we need to talk."

Marylee opened the door and walked behind the small desk with the glass top and sat down. The office was small, the lighting was dim, the room dark and depressing. Rev. Dinkins pulled up a chair and sat across from her. "Talk to me Marylee. Tell me what's going on?"

Marylee looked at her husband of more than eighteen years and thought, how little he really knew about her and her life before him. She decided not to tell him everything, but enough.

Marylee opened the side door of the cabinet behind her desk and pulled out a bottle of Jack Daniels and two glasses. She poured the whiskey into the glasses and moved one of them toward Rev. Dinkins. She picked up her glass and slowly took a sip of the whiskey. She turned toward the window and decided to get up and let some light into the room. It was still light outside, and the sun was still shining. As she stood there looking out of the narrow window at nothing in particular, she began to craft the story she wanted to tell Rev. Dinkins. The whiskey she poured for her husband sat there staring him in the face. He remembered the last time he needed a drink; that night in 1939 when he and Brownie had the accident that killed 16 people.

Marylee turned around and began. "Richard, my grandmother who lived in Baton Rue Louisiana was a practicing voodoo master. We were told she was a slave but always considered herself free. The slave master was afraid of her because he felt she was owned by the devil and had powers that he did not have. He felt she would cast a spell on him and his family. So, he gave her whatever she wanted including a baby and her freedom. My mother was the daughter from that union and my mother's father (the slave owner) was burned to death in a voodoo ceremony conducted by my grandmother."

"What the hell does this have to do with Kizzy's kidnapping?" Rev. Dinkins snapped with a booming voice. "Did you take the girl? Did you take her? I'm tired of your lies. Do you really expect me to listen to this bullshit?" Unconscious of his actions, Richard Dinkins reached for the small half-filled glass of whiskey and without thinking, he quickly drank the whiskey. Marylee smiled slyly. She knew he would take the bait.

"No, I don't expect you to believe me. But I want you to try to understand why I think the girl is missing. And, no, I didn't kidnap little Kizzy." Marylee was about to continue, but before she did, she poured them both another drink. What she was about to say would change their lives forever.

"My mother's grandmother made a deal with the devil. In exchange for deeper powers and connections with the dark world of witchcraft and voodoo she offered the soul of my mother's firstborn girl to the devil. My mother took part in the ceremony when I was born, and my soul was sold to the devil. Throughout my childhood and early teens, I practiced voodoo. When you and I met in New York, I was on a mission for an organization called the Shadow. The Shadow deals in predictable behavior information trafficking. My assignment was to marry you and make sure you and Brownie Caldwell met. Several psychics who worked at Shadow had visions of a girl who would be born in Harrisburg, PA around 1945. The girl would have extraordinary powers and gifts over her lifetime that could destroy everything the Shadow built. They needed the girl for the survival of the organization. The psychics could only predict the family the child would be born into and the birthday. A representative from the Shadow Corporation stayed in close contact with me for years to help determine if Kizzy was the one. On Monday, they contacted me again. After seven years they were ready for the girl.

Why they left the dead animal in the church or where they took Kizzy, I don't know."

Richard Dinkins looked at his wife and without a word, he got up and walked to the door. He turned around and said, "I'm going to pick up the kids. We won't be coming back tonight. Pack your things and be gone by noon tomorrow. You are dead to me." He opened the door and walked out.

Marylee was not sad. Richard Dinkins was finally out of her life. She had pretended for so long to enjoy the life they were building in Harrisburg. She enjoyed the power of leading a large church and having influence over so many vulnerable men and women but the chance for freedom from him and the children excited her.

Richard had given her until noon to leave. Marylee decided that was just enough time for her to send a signal to Shadow and let them know her assignment in Harrisburg was over. She would go to the connect point in New York to wait for what was next. She could now practice her craft without the constraints of what Richard preached and the church stood for. She had no feelings of love for him or the children; they were all a means to an end and part of an assignment.

The Shadow Corporation paid well. They always paid at the end of an assignment whether the assignment was successful or not. Marylee was thinking how close she was to bringing them a prize (the Caldwell girl) and regaining her soul. The only regret had been not fulfilling her mission to cease the power promised to her by her mother. She had an idea who had kidnapped Kizzy. She feared the girl would enter the Landing organization and become the powerful force Shadow Corporation feared. The craft of her mother, grandmother and great-grandmother was the only way out for Marylee, and why she was recruited in the Shadow organization years ago.

Thursday, Afternoon, May 8

Rev. Dinkins was preoccupied by his thoughts when he walked out of the church front door and approached by an excited man and woman who lived in the neighborhood.

"Good Afternoon, Reverend Dinkins, did you hear the news?"

"What news?" Rev. Dinkins asked.

"The news about Brownie Caldwell's daughter, Kizzy," the man replied. Rev. Dinkins swallowed hard. The man continued, "they found the girl."

"Where is she?" Richard asked.

"Well, I'm not exactly sure. I just ran into old Jack who works in the candy store across the street from the Caldwell's house. Jack told me a lot of people are over there now. Sounds like some college boys found the girl down there in Hershey or Lancaster. I'm not sure." The man looked at his wife for support; she nodded her head up and down in agreement.

The man's wife added, "Please be sure to let Ms. Marylee know, she really liked that little girl, and no one blames her for what happened at the church."

Rev. Dinkins nodded and replied, "Well, I appreciate the news. Thank you for letting me know. And I'll be sure to let Marylee know."

Rev. Dinkins didn't know exactly what to think or do. His immediate instinct was to go back in the church and share with Marylee what he just heard. But he stopped himself and decided to call Brownie instead to see if the rumor was true. He still had his own business to tend to before the day was over. And he and Brownie needed to finalize the funeral plans for Emily Caldwell. Marylee would not be there to help him. He would call Kara, Emily's sister for help, they had developed a close relationship over the years, and he trusted her with his most private thoughts.

The telephone was ringing in Richard's office, the only phone in the church; Marylee was closing the door to her office and carrying a box with her personal belongings. Margie, a lady friend from the church, was coming to pick her up. The phone kept ringing. Marylee decided to pick it up just in case it was Margie calling. She put the box down and went into Richard's office.

"Hello, Living Word Gospel Church, may I help you?"

There was a moment of silence then a familiar voice said, "Marylee this is Brownie, I got some good news! They just bought Kizzy home. I'm going down to the hospital now to see her. Is Richard around?"

Marylee was speechless.

"Marylee, are you still there?"

"Yes Brownie, I'm here." She could hear her breathing. "Is Kizzy okay?"

"Yes, I think so, we got the call from the police that she's at the hospital. They believe she was given some kind of drug, but she should be okay. Some college kids found her at an old farm near Hershey. I don't know much more. Is Richard there?"

Marylee hesitated for a few seconds then she said, "No, Brownie, Richard left about fifteen minutes ago. I'll let him know you called."

"Okay, thanks Marylee. Oh, Marylee I'm ready to finish the funeral arrangements for Emily's funeral, so I'll see you soon."

Marylee didn't say anything; she just hung-up the phone. Margie was standing in the doorway. "You look like you are packing up. What's going on?"

Marylee looked at Margie and said, "I've been called to a higher calling. I'm going to meet my destiny."

Chapter 6

Clay and Mason

C lay and Mason drove up the dusty graveled road toward the farmhouse. The darkness and long day of shooting pictures, discussing their future and their early college days gave way to two very tired young men. Clay looked straight ahead as he drove the car, his left arm resting on the open window ledge. He was thinking about the cold beer in back of the car and the good night's sleep that awaited him at the farmhouse. Mason was fiddling with the radio, turning from the country western station to something more soulful. Mason was finally done turning the channel when he looked up.

"WATCH OUT!" Mason yelled. Clay made a sudden turn that landed the car in a ditch. "Did you see that?" Mason steadied himself against the dashboard.

"Holy Shit. What is that?" Clay asked, his hands still tightly gripping the steering wheel.

Mason was silent as he stared at the figures dancing in a circle in front of him on the open road.

Both men starred at the halo that bounced off the gravel stones from the car's headlights. Slowly the halo began to disappear, Clay and Mason looked at each other, realizing they had witnessed something really strange.

"Unbelievable. I don't think I've ever seen anything like that before. What are they? Aliens or spirits?" Clay whispered. An hour passed. Both men had fallen asleep or were hypnotized as they watched the unusual signs. When they awoke, the figures were gone and they were in the car but on the side of the road, not in a ditch.

Clay turned to look at Mason who was still sleeping with his head and arm resting against the window. Clay reached over and shook him lightly. Mason turned and looked at Clay, disoriented or not sure where he was.

"Whew, I can't believe we fell asleep on the side of the road like this. And man, I had this weird dream about aliens," Clay said in a bewildered and uncertain voice.

"So did I. It was so real," Mason said. "You were in my dreams and a little colored girl was there with us, and I believe they were aliens."

Clay interrupted with renewed energy. "I saw her too; she was in the car with us. We were taking her somewhere special." Clay shook his head and continued, "We were in a ditch and these aliens or spirts were dancing in a circle with the little girl. Mason, this may sound crazy, but I saw myself as a much older man holding hands with the same beautiful colored woman. Can you believe that? My parents would disown me if they ever thought I would date a colored girl."

Mason was silent as he listened to Clay. He too had dreamed about holding hands with a colored woman. How weird they had the same dream, or was this something more?

Clay Barksdale, Jr. was twenty-one years old, graduating in two weeks from Princeton. His plans were to complete a tour of duty in the Air Force and afterwards enter Yale for law school and then work at one of his family's businesses as a corporate attorney. He had a girlfriend who he met during his freshman year. Allison Rankin was a senior too with plans of entering med school later in the summer. Allison's family and the Barksdale family were major investors in Landing Enterprises. The families wanted nothing more than to hear that Allison and Clay were engaged. However, Clay wasn't sure Allison was the one for him.

Mason Johnson was twenty-one years old, scheduled to graduate with Clay from Princeton in two weeks. He too had been accepted into the Air Force Academy and planned to make a career out of the military. His interest was engineering, and he had plans to attend MIT. He was seriously dating someone for the past three years and planned to pop the question during the Christmas holidays. She was Clay's youngest sister, Meredith Barksdale, a junior at Barnard.

Mason was uneasy about the relationship from the start. Mixed-race relationships and marriages were generally frowned upon, and Mason knew the relationship with

Meredith had the potential to end his long friendship with Clay, a conservative from Pennsylvania.

Mason had grown up in Washington D.C., and the family moved several times as his father was a career military man serving in US Air Force. His mother was trained as a teacher and sub-teacher became her career. Mason was an only child. Making friends was easy for him and he was good at it. His parents always saw Mason as a lawyer or public servant and were surprised he wanted to become an engineer. The also wondered why he never brought any girls home to meet them, although there were signs he was dating someone. They wondered why all the secrecy about the girl he was dating.

Both young men saw this time together as more than just an adventure. They needed to talk about their friendship and life after graduation.

"Mason, do you trust me?" Clay asked. "I need to tell you something about my family and share with you why your relationship with my sister will never work. Meredith told me everything."

Mason was shocked to learn Meredith had confided in Clay after they had discussed Mason's plans to talk with Clay during this trip to the Barksdale Farms. When did she tell him and why?

Clay turned the radio off as he glanced over to look at Mason whose face he could not fully see because of the darkness of the night. The car went silent with a distinct air of tension.

"What do want me to say? If Meredith told you everything. I had planned to tell you tonight about our marriage plans and ask you to be my best man. I hoped you would be happy for us. Meredith and I love each other. I'm not marrying your parents. This will not be easy for my parents either, but I am counting on you to be there for us."

"Man, I feel betrayed," Clay blurted you. "You dated my sister for three years and never said a word. I watched you with other girls on campus and listened to your stories about the future and what you wanted and did not want. We talked race relations, our families, segregation, and the law.

"You are the only one I talked to about Allison and why it would never work between the two of us. I trusted our friendship and thought it meant as much to you as it did me. Yet, I feel betrayed. You should have told me." The car was turning a slight bend in the road. The moon was full, and its bright light lit up the car. Clay could finally see Mason's face. There was nothing there. He stared blankly out of the window, appearing far away in his own thoughts.

In front of them on the hill stood the old farmhouse glowing with a full moon in the background. They were finally back from a long day trip.

Clay parked the car off to the side of the house. The silence remained. The men got out of the car, and both noticed something peculiar on the front porch.

"Hello! Someone there?" Clay called out. Mason walked beside Clay and both boys looked at each other and shrugged their shoulders.

"Are you thinking what I'm thinking?" Mason asked Clay as they continued to walk to the front of the house.

Clay responded, "You mean what we saw on the road earlier or in our dreams?" The boys walked up the steps and that's when their lives would change forever.

"Oh my God. Is there a body on the porch?" Clay said as he reached out to touch the blanket. They could only see a small head half covered and small feet with white bobby socks poking out from the bottom of the covering. The covering was a beautiful purple and gold cloth of some kind.

"Clay, don't touch anything. Be careful! We need to call the police. Is there a working phone in the house?" Mason asked as he too leaned over the bundle on the porch.

"Yeah, it's hidden but I was told it would work," Clay replied as both men stood up.

In a surprised voice, Mason said, "Did you see something moving under the coverings? Oh my god."

The moon appeared at its fullest, seeming to engulf the entire farmhouse in its aura. The body under the blanket turned fully to face Clay and Mason. Kizzy's face was full of light as the moon shone brightly across her face, and the boys were mesmerized and in shock. They had never seen anyone more beautiful. Then she opened her eyes and looked at the two men standing in front of her. In that magical moment all three of them saw images of themselves together holding hands.

Clay experienced in that moment a feeling of joy he had never felt before and visions of the young colored woman he had dreamt about not only on the road today, but several times before was more real to him at this moment than ever.

Mason felt peace and a sense of resolution about his decision to marry Meredith. Although the woman he met on the road earlier tonight, the woman who haunted him in dreams – he had to find her. She was his destiny.

"Where are Eula and Iva?" a frightened Kizzy asked the two speechless young men in front of her as she unwrapped herself from the blanket and tried to stand. She tried to stand and started to fall but Clay caught her. She was a bit off balance, and her vision was blurred from the large amount of drugs Iva had given her earlier. She was shaking badly and had wetted herself from hours of not using a bathroom. She was very weak. "Mason, open the door and let's get this little girl inside," Clay ordered as the two boys cautiously moved inside house. "Somebody else was here. Why did they leave the little girl? Who is she? Who are Eula and Iva?"

"Do you think the little girl is okay?" Mason asked. "Is she sick? We need to call the police. People will think we kidnapped this kid. Do you know how much trouble we will be in? I can't believe this is happening to us."

"Mason, I think she's asleep. I'm going to light a fire. Here, let's put her over here near the fire. I'll get some pillows from the bedroom and get the phone. Go check out the back of the house and I'll look around here."

"Okay, I'm on it," Mason said, relieved to have something concrete to do.

Clay found the phone and dialed the operator. "Hello, this is the operator. May I help you?"

"Hello, my name is Clay Barksdale. Please connect me with the police. We have an emergency out at the old Barksdale Farm."

"Sir, what did you say your name was?"

"Clay Barksdale."

"One moment, sir. We are connecting you now to the local police."

Clay looked over at the little girl and noticed Mason was building a fire. The girl was asleep. The house had signs of recent guests. Who was there while they were gone?

"Hello, Lancaster County police department, Lt. Malone here. Can I help you?"

"Yes, yes, my name is Clay Barksdale. I am out at the old Barksdale farmhouse. My friend and I just returned tonight from a field trip, and we found a little colored girl on the front porch."

"Slow down young man. Is everyone okay?"

"No, I mean I'm not sure. The little girl looks like something is wrong with her."

"Where is the girl now?"

"She's here in the house now with me and my friend, asleep on the floor."

"Is anyone else there in the house with you and your friend?"

"No, we don't think anyone else is here now. We believe someone might have been here earlier while we were away."

"Okay, what did you say your name was again?"

"Clay Barksdale."

"Are you old man Barksdale's grandson?"

"Yes, that's my granddad. How soon before someone can get here? The little girl may need medical attention."

"Mr. Barksdale, we'll get someone over there as soon as possible. It's the middle of the night and we have to call over to Harrisburg for help."

"How long do you think that will take?"

"Couple hours at the most. Doesn't sound like an emergency."

"Hello? Hello? Hello! Damn it, did he hang up? Oh, the phone is dead. No connection."

"What happened? Are they coming?" Mason's voice was anxious. He too was concerned about the girl and wondered what they could do to help her. The strangest thing was both Clay and Mason felt a special bond with this little girl, and they wanted to do whatever they could to make sure she was okay.

Clay was angry. "I'm not sure! There was no urgency in their voices. Not sure if they thought this was a prank call or what. I just hope they hurry and get their asses over here. If not, let's drive the girl to the hospital. Something's not right with her."

"Uhm, why don't we wait until the morning and see how she does overnight, then take her. She seems cold and sleepy. Maybe being inside close to a warm fire will help. Plus, by morning the police might be here by then."

"She asked about Elua and Iva. I wonder who that might be?" Clay asked.

"Maybe those are the people who bought her here. But why would they leave her? Doesn't make any sense." Mason sat at the table and opened a beer. Clay unpacked the bag he had brought into the house. He was still worried and questioning the decision not to take the girl to the hospital right away. He walked over to the table where Mason was sitting, pulled up a chair, and sat down.

Both of the young men were restless. There was so much they needed to talk about, but now with the girl, their life had just become a bit more complicated.

Mason started, "Clay, I was going to tell you about me and Meredith, but it never seemed like the right time. When your father got sick, it changed things. Your entire family was worried about him, and I just couldn't add to the family stress. When did Meredith tell you about us?"

Clay looked at Mason. He saw someone who he really cared for and treated like the brother he never had. Clay knew Meredith would never marry Mason. She would never risk her social status and money for love. She was too insecure to take that risk. Meredith was too blue-blooded to let love override money, but he could not and would not tell Mason his family were all racists and would never accept him into the family.

They were too tired to eat. They looked over at the girl who was curled up on the floor on the blanket they found her in next to a nice warm fire. Mason added another log to the fire as the boys fell silent and started to nod off. Clay struggled to sleep. He kept his eyes on the girl while thinking about Allison. How would he tell her it was over? He never intended for it to end this way. There was nothing there, no feelings, nothing. He lost the desire for her a long time ago. She was replaced in his dreams and thoughts by the mystery woman who haunted his dreams. He drifted off to sleep with thoughts of his mystery woman.

Mason struggled to sleep too. He slowly got up to go to the bathroom. The girl was asleep, and Clay was sleeping too. Mason noticed the case on the bathroom floor and wondered what was inside. He was too tired to look. He would take a look in the morning.

He walked out of the bathroom to the kitchen. He was thirsty and decided to open a can of beer and sit out on the front porch. He checked to make sure the girl was still asleep, then opened the door and sat on the steps of the porch. The night air was cool. It was quiet, and the sky was full of stars. He wondered why Meredith told Clay about their relationship.

Mason knew an interracial marriage would be difficult for both families, but he loved Meredith and was willing to give life with her a chance. He wondered if she was as committed as he was. There were signs she wasn't sure. Mason wanted to get married in the fall before he left for the military. Meredith wanted to wait a few more years, at least until she finished her first couple years of medical school. Mason sat there sipping his beer, leaning against the railing and staring into the vast darkness that engulfed the old country road.

Wednesday, May 8, the next morning

Kizzy pulled the blanket off her face and slowly tried to sit up from her resting place on a dark brown shag rug near the fireplace. She was dizzy, a throbbing pounding headache had developed, and her stomach was in knots. The last thing she remembered was Iva putting a needle in her arm, but she couldn't remember anything after that.

Kizzy's vision was a bit blurred, but she could see the shadows in front of her. When her eyes became clearer, she saw the two men in the room. A skinny white man with dark hair was sleeping on the old beige three-cushioned couch facing the fireplace. The other man was colored, but she wasn't sure because he was awfully light, just like her uncle Smithy. He was stretched out on the oversized wooden framed recliner positioned on the other side of the fireplace. Kizzy would later learn their names were Clay and Mason.

"Ms. Eula, Ms. Iva where are you? Mrs. Eula, Mrs. Iva, I'M SCARED somebody in this house!" Kizzy yelled as she ran toward the door.

Clay snapped awake and Mason heard the voice screaming too.

"It's okay. Its okay," Mason said. "My name is Mason."

Kizzy moved away from him. "Ms. Iva Ms. Eula!" Kizzy called out. Tears began to stream down her face, frightened and confused as to where she was and who these men where. She stood in the middle of the room and just screamed. There was nowhere to go.

Mason walked around Clay and stood a few inches from Kizzy. Mason was thinking the maybe he could make the girl feel more comfortable since he too was colored. "Hello, my name is Mason. What's your name?"

Kizzy did not respond. She stood there crying, shaking, and positioned behind an old chair next to the fireplace.

Mason continued. "Hey, let me help you. We are not here to hurt you. Are you okay? And where did you come from? Who are Eula and Iva?"

Kizzy cried softly as she hovered behind the chair. Her body tensed with fear. She had that feeling again, the one she always felt right before something "big" was about to happen to her. Kizzy fell to the floor and called out, "GOD help me …. Help me please! YOU promised to take care of me. Please – I need you now. You promised!"

Then there was silence. The girl lay on the floor behind the old wooden chair, motionless.

Clay and Mason were stunned by the child's plea, not exactly a cry or a frightened person's plea but a matter-of-fact urgent request for something the child believed she could ask. Both of the boys looked at each other and were motionless. What could they do?

Clay leaned next the pole that anchored the kitchen counter, wondering where did this girl come from and how long would it take before the police got her to talk.

"Are you hungry?" Mason asked Kizzy. Kizzy kept crying and did not respond to his question. "Hey Clay,"

Mason yelled, "bring me an orange juice and donut from the A&P bag."

Clay moved toward to cooler to get the juice. He was concerned for the girl and hoping he and Mason could get her to talk. He began to look around the kitchen. That's when he saw the envelope on the counter next to the sink. Clay wondered what an envelope was doing on the sink counter.

"Uhm…." He whispered the words on the front of the envelop "OPEN and READ IMMEDIATELY. What the F…K!" Clay leaned over the sink and opened the envelope. There were three words written on a piece of paper inside. Kizzy, Harrisburg, Perch. Clay shrugged his shoulders and shoved the piece paper crossed the counter.

"Clay, man, what's taking you so long?" Mason yelled. He was getting restless watching the scared little girl. The little girl was very scared. She just lay there staring straight ahead at nothing. Mason thought at nothing particular.

"Here you go." Clay put the orange juice and donut on the table next to the chair. He stood next to Mason. "How do you think she's doing?"

"I'm not sure. She's quiet but seem to be in some type of mental state we need to get her out of here and to a hospital. Man, I'm scared. Do you realize how much trouble we might be in with this little girl here alone with us? Clay, we got to figure something out."

"Yea, I agree. This is not looking good. No one is going to believe we found this girl here alone. We got to figure this out. How old do you think she is?"

"Seven or eight. Hard to tell she's so petite. We need to get her to eat and drink something. Her name and where she's from. We need to find the ladies she asked for, what were their names?"

"No clue. Seems like that was a long time ago, and it was just minutes ago. By the way, what took you so long in the kitchen?"

Clay thought for a minute. "Mason, I was opening an envelope that was on the kitchen counter that had a piece paper inside with three words."

Clay walked toward the kitchen to get the piece of paper. He bought it back to the main room and read the words out loud slowly breathing after each word. "KIZZY. HARRISBURG. PERCH."

Mason tapped Clay on the forearm and motioned for him to turn around.

The little girl was standing behind them. Clay turned around to meet the girl's eyes; they were dark and empty; yet beautiful. He was surprised when she spoke.

"Will you take me home? The watcher told me you would take me," Kizzy said.

Clay was speechless. He almost felt like he was under a spell. He looked into the little girl's eyes and felt an unexplainable connection and closeness that scared him. She was a child, but his feelings were adult feeling. Then he spoke her name.

"Kizzy?"

Kizzy nodded her head to signal yes. She then walked over to the chair, sat down, reached for the orange juice and donut and began to hum.

Mason was almost in shock watching the exchange between the little girl and Clay. Mason nudged Clay as if to shake him from a trance. "Clay, you okay? Hey you okay?"

"I'm okay, but Mason, we need to go."

"Go where?"

"Harrisburg."

The boys started gathering only their backpacks. They would leave everything else there for their return. Harrisburg wasn't that far away. But they would take enough for a day trip just in case they needed to stay longer in Harrisburg. Neither of them knew what to expect.

The old Ford truck pulled up in back of the old Chevy and parked. The boys did not hear truck drive up. Inside of the truck sat Clay's grandfather, Winston Clay Barksdale. The Police Lt. had given him a call to relate the conversation they had with his grandson about the little girl they found inside the farmhouse.

Winston Barksdale didn't know what to expect. He loved his grandson and would do whatever he had to do to protect him. Old man Barksdale got out of the truck and walked up the steps and tried to look in one of the few windows. He could not see anything. He knocked on the door.

Mason opened the door. The two men greeted each other with coldness and disdain. Mason could only see an old man with built-up hatred and bias for anyone and anything different from him. Mr. Barksdale saw in Mason a major roadblock to everything he envisioned for his grandson. Now, this entanglement with a little girl. Mr. Barksdale was fuming and his hatred for Mason only grew more intense in those few seconds. Mason moved aside as Mr. Barksdale crossed the threshold. Mr. Barksdale represented everything he was taught about racism. He could not help but think of Meredith. How was she going to tell her family about them. Of course, telling Clay was a good first step.

Kizzy had finished her orange juice and donut. She was looking for the gifts from Eula and Iva. She remembered. Maybe in her dreams that they had given her a small box and told her to open it only on her birthday. They asked Kizzy to promise to wait and open it then. She promised them she would wait. Kizzy remembered Iva covering the box with the blue sweater that Iva had worn the night they walked along the river. Kizzy had to find the sweater. She was on her hands and knees crawling across the floor looking under the old couch when Mr. Barksdale walked in. Clay was in the bathroom and nowhere in sight, but he heard his grandfather's loud booming voice.

"What the hell is going on in here? Clay Barksdale! Where are you, boy?" He turned again to Mason and asked, "Where's my grandson? What kind of trouble have you gotten him into? What is that colored girl doing crawling on the floor?"

Before Mason could say anything, Clay was back in the main room and reaching out to hug his grandfather.

"Grandpa, how you doing? I could hear you calling for me all the way in the john… How did you know I was here?" Clay asked.

"Well, I got a call from my friends over at the police station. They told me there might be some trouble out here. So, I packed my gun and drove over to see what's going on. You look okay?" Winston Barksdale said.

"Grandpa I'm fine. You know Mason," Clay said.

Winston Barksdale nodded in acknowledgment in Mason's direction.

Mr. Barksdale stepped back as Kizzy came closer to him and Mason remained near the front door leaning against the wall with his head tilted and eyes staring at the ceiling, listening to Clay reason with the old man, trying to calm him.

"What are these colored people doing on Barksdale property and who is that girl?" Mr. Barksdale asked in a frustrated tone, as if his grandson should know better and had forgotten the rules of the Barksdale family.

"Let me explain, Grandpa. Now sit down," Clay said.

Clay always had a knack for calming his grandfather and explaining things in a way that at least his grandfather would listen. Winston Barksdale always had a counter punch, was brutally honest with his opinions and thoughts. And yet he and Clay had this amazing relationship since he was a little boy and it continued throughout Clay four years at Princeton.

Mr. Barksdale believed his grandson Clay Barksdale Jr. would one day become a great lawyer and politician. He just worried about Clay's political views and was concerned that

Clay was not conservative enough for a political career in Pennsylvania. Mr. Barksdale always saw those damn liberal tendencies in Clay as just like his uncle's, Robert Barksdale (the eldest son) in Philadelphia and his grandmother, Karen Weinstock's (on his mother's side), in New York. Sending Clay to Princeton certainly didn't help with his liberal leanings.

"Kizzy, come here, I want to introduce you to my grandfather, Mr. Barksdale," Clay said.

Clay reached out for Kizzy's hand. Instead, the girl turned away from Clay and moved closer to Winston Barksdale. She looked him straight in the face with the confidence and maturity that surpassed her young age.

Mr. Barksdale extended his hand to the little girl without thinking.

"How do you do little missy?" He said to Kizzy, shocking himself and Clay.

Kizzy smiled slightly. "I'm fine, sir. You can call me Kiz Lamise Caldwell. But friends and family call me Kizzy."

Winston Barksdale paused a moment. He was thinking the name was familiar.

"Caldwell, Caldwell, Caldwell. Over there in Harrisburg," Winston Barksdale repeated as he turned to look at his grandson, Clay.

"Son, is this is the little colored girl missing from Harrisburg? The entire county is looking for her. How? What's going on Clay!"

Clay looked over at Mason. Mason came closer to the three of them and unfolded his arms and sat on the edge of the fireplace. Kizzy sat on the floor near the corner of the couch, Clay and his grandfather sat on the old couch together, pillow seats sinking low, the room pleasantly light, the temperature just right, the sounds of their voices and breathing was the only sound heard.

Then the voice of a little girl began.

"My mom looked at me before she died and said, 'Don't be sad, Kizzy, the watchman will always protect you. Let me go.' Her head was in my lap, the blood dripped all over my yellow and black skirt, I couldn't help but cry.

"I looked down at her, her eyes were still open, and she was looking at something far away. Mom's hands were at first wrapped around my legs as if she didn't want me to go. I could hear her say, 'Kizzy stop running. Stop running. Stop running.' Then her arms fell slowly against the old brick steps and my legs felt like chains had been removed. She was gone; I was sad but not afraid. I lifted my mom's head from my lap and placed it on the step. When I stood up her blood was all over my new socks and shoes.

"The watcher told me the men who killed my mom were coming for me. My mom did not let them know I was home. She had something else they wanted that only I can give them. The blue and white car that I saw from the window was like the one at school the day the burned-up men were on the ground. The burned-up men looked at Colin, my friend, and me and said, 'Run Kizzy, Run Kizzy.'"

Mason interrupted Kizzy and asked, "How did you get here?"

Both Winston Barksdale and Clay shot a look at Mason, like why did you stop her from telling the story?

Clay immediately stood up. He remembered the words on the piece of paper. Kizzy... Harrisburg... Perch. He walked to the kitchen and put the piece of paper in his pocket. Clay was trying to put the pieces together. It would take almost 20 years before the meaning of the Perch would be clear to Clay.

Mr. Barksdale stood up too and walked to the kitchen. He summoned Mason over too.

"Clay, I'm not sure what's going on. But the tension in Harrisburg right now is really bad. The word is some white men killed the Caldwell woman, killed some other folks and somebody kidnapped the Caldwell girl, or she ran away," Winston Barksdale said.

He continued to share with Clay and Mason what happened in Harrisburg that week. The boys had no idea.

"You boys could be in a lot of trouble. I don't want you involved in the mess. I'll take the girl to Harrisburg and tell the police I found here alone in my old farmhouse. I have a lot of friends in Harrisburg and few of the police here owe me some favors too. You boys need to get out of here and get on up there to school and let me handle this. The little girl is a great storyteller. Not sure how much of her story people will believe," Winston Barksdale said.

"Grandpa… I'm going with you," Clay said in a matter-of-fact way.

"Clay, maybe you should listen to your grandfather, I think he's making a lot of sense."

Mason continued, "We shouldn't get involved. This does not look good for us. How are we going to explain where we've been over the last several days and why? No one is going to believe we didn't have anything do with the little girl's disappearance. And we still don't know how she got here."

"Clay, Mason is right. You boys will be in a lot of trouble with the town's people and the police up there in Harrisburg. We need to get to a phone. Is the old phone in the closet working?" Mr. Barksdale walked over to the closet to check on the phone.

Clay was thinking. Something is not adding up. Why did his grandfather come all the way out here by himself? And, why he was not concerned that the placed looked lived-in beyond the time the boys arrived. Why did he not question how the little girl found her way to his farmhouse?

Something was off. Clay knew his grandfather, and this was not his normal pattern of thinking. Plus, someone had charged the phone before they got there… How did they know where to find the phone? Who was his grandfather calling? Clay was almost overwhelmed with uneasiness and questions. He also noticed his grandfather's intense focus on the girl, as if she was a prize he had just won.

"What are you thinking?" Mason asked as he turned toward Clay.

"What do you think? Should we get the hell out of here and head back to Princeton?" Clay asked.

"I'll do whatever you want to do, man. But we need to be really sure," Mason said.

Kizzy walked into the kitchen and asked for another donut. Mason reached into the A&P bag and handed her another donut, a bag of chips, and an apple. She smiled and walked back to the main room. The boys realized they were hungry too, so they both raided the A&P bag for junk food.

Grandpa Barksdale found the phone box. After he figured out how to get the old thing working, he dialed the emergency number he kept in his wallet. The private number for the local police chief.

"Hello Chief." There was silence on the other end.

"Ed, is that you." Winston Barksdale repeated.

"Hello, Winston, sounds like you are up at the farm. How are things there?" the police chief asked.

"Not so good. Ed, I need your help. The Caldwell girl is at my place."

"Caldwell... Caldwell... You mean the missing colored girl from Harrisburg?" Ed asked with surprise.

"Yea. She's seemed okay. But my grandson Clay is mixed up in this somehow. I got to get my grandson as far away from this mess as possible." Winston continued.

"Ed, this damn phone is not worth shit. I'm losing connection. Come on up to the farm. We got to get this girl out of here as soon as possible."

"Winston, I'm on my way. I'll be over there in 30 minutes. Should I bring Jake or make a call to the others?" Ed asked.

"No, you come alone, and we'll handle this ourselves. Damn it! This worthless piece of shit of phone."

Winston Barksdale returned to the room as Clay, Mason and Kizzy were about to open the front door. Clay turned around to face his grandfather as Kizzy and Mason continued to walk out of the door.

"Clay this is nonsense. You are about to ruin your life over this colored girl. Let me handle this. I have some people already on the way. We'll take care of everything. No one will ever know that you and Mason were ever here. Both of you can go on with your life."

"Grandfather… she's going home. I don't know what happened to her or how she ended up here, but we are leaving and somehow, I feel it's my responsibility to make sure she's safe. I hope you have nothing to do with any of this."

Winston Barksdale watched his beloved grandson walk out of the door and wondered what the boy knew and if he would ever see him again. It wasn't supposed to be this way; Clay was his oldest grandson and he planned to leave everything to him. He looked as the back of the old Chevy slowly disappeared in the dust. There was so much he wanted to share with Clay while he was still alive – there wasn't much time to tell him the truth about the Barksdale fortune and his birthright.

Wednesday evening, May 8

Clay, Mason, and Kizzy were headed to Harrisburg. Clay was anxious to get off the rough country road to the paved highway. He needed to relax. Mason was talking to Kizzy about her family. He overheard her say, "I don't have a family, they are all gone."

"Gone, gone where?" Mason asked.

"I don't know. They just all went away." Kizzy's voice began to fade.

"What about a game?" Clay interrupted, trying to lighten the mood and make the girl more comfortable.

"Oh no, not a game, let's sing a song," Kizzy said, her voice gaining strength again as she leaned from the back floor mount between the middle arm rest, her face perched on her hands and looking at Clay and Mason.

"Go ahead and pick a song, Kizzy, we'll join in," Clay said with a curious tone.

Kizzy began in a beautiful, angelic, soprano voice, "This little light of mine, I'm gonna let it shine, let it shine, let it shine everywhere I go. This little light of mine I'm gone to let it shine. Let it shine, let it shine, let it shine."

She stopped and looked at both Clay and Mason. "What's wrong, don't you like my song?"

Clay didn't say anything.

"Yes, I know your song," Mason said. "I learned it in Sunday school when I was a little boy." He looked at Clay and knew they needed to pick a different song.

Kizzy sensed the boys did not like her song. "Do you want to sing a different song with me?"

Clay nodded and so did Mason.

"Okay. I'll teach you the words to my favorite song. I wrote this song for the Watchman… my very special friend."

Clay turned to Mason who was now turned all the way around in the car looking at Kizzy; he was hoping they would soon see the exit sign to Harrisburg. He was getting tired and thinking about his grandfather and how he would make amends with the old man. He felt Kizzy tapping him on the shoulder.

"Do you want to learn the words to my special song?" Kizzy waited for Clay to nod his head in agreement. She then began.

"First, I will say the words out loud, then you will repeat the words after me. And when you know the words, we will sing. I will help you."

Mason nodded and started to smile. He was really curious what her song was about. Who was the watchman? She was an amazing little girl. Seeing her full of energy and excitement meant this song was pretty special to her.

Kizzy tapped Clay again and asked in a joyful voice, "Will you say the words too?"

Clay smiled but kept his eyes on the road. "Yes, I will say the words and sing too."

Kizzy was jumping up and down on the back seat. She was so happy. After a few seconds she settled down and leaned forward again. She began, "Okay listen to the words;

first we'll say them together then we'll sing. It's my special song."

She began.

"Wake me in the morning, afternoon, or night, anytime to let me you are here. I need you, I need you and I want you near. Can you hear my cry can you hear my cry. Please let me know you still care. Do I dare tell a soul you love me? Wake me when you are here."

The car was entering the exit to Harrisburg as Kizzy was ending. Clay made a sharp turn as he entered the exit to avoid hitting a stalled car. The unexpected jerk caused Kizzy to hit her head slightly on the back of the driver seat and Mason's shoulder hit the dashboard before he was able to brace himself. Clay was okay.

"Whew... that was close," Clay said out loud as he turned to check on Kizzy. "Are you okay," he asked?

Kizzy nodded.

"Are those people okay?" Mason asked out loud as he opened the car door. "Stay in the car," he turned and instructed Kizzy. Clay got out of the car too and both Clay and Mason walked over to the other car to make sure the people on the car were okay.

Kizzy sat on the back seat and sang softly to herself. "I need you. I need you and I want you near. Can you hear my cry can you hear my cry. Please let me know you still care."

Mason and Clay saw an elderly couple sitting inside the stalled truck. Then they saw the teenaged boy on the other side of the truck and the rubber from a blown-out tire on the side of the exit.

"Hey, can we help you?" Clay called out to the teenaged boy who appeared to be changing a tire.

The boy looked up.

Kizzy Homecoming

The call was the best news Brownie could ever have received. His baby girl was okay. The police were bringing her home from the hospital. So many thoughts were going through his head, and he was overwhelmed with emotions. He would bury his wife within 24 hours and his children's future was uncertain; they had all been impacted by the events of the week.

The drive to Harrisburg was shorter than Clay remembered it as a child. Mason and Clay talked about what possibly could happen to them. But neither of them cared. They were doing the right thing.

Kizzy was excited during most of trip. She sang songs out loud and talked to an imaginary friend. She was in her own world.

They arrived in Harrisburg around 11:00 am on a beautiful Friday morning. The boys had decided to go directly to the police station with the girl. The police Chief Raymond Kelly received the call from Hershey's Lt. Jake that the girl was on the way. They were told the boys were not responsible for her disappearance. They found her at the Barksdale

Farm when they returned from a camping trip. They believed two women named Eula and Iva were responsible for her disappearance. The women may be headed to Philadelphia or New York based on additional information received by their sources.

When Clay and Mason brough her in, the chief spoke to her directly. "Welcome home, Kizzy. We are so happy to see you. Before we do anything else, we want to have our doctors check you out to make sure everything is okay. I'm sure you are hungry too."

The Police Chief gestured toward his assistant, an older woman name Connie Bell to call over to Harrisburg Hospital to let them know he was personally bringing the girl over for a thorough check-up.

"Please call my daddy. I want to go home," Kizzy said in a weak voice with a stream of tears falling down her face. "Will you call my dad? My telephone is Cedar 236-8556." She repeated the phone number again as she was taught so many times: "Cedar 236-8556."

Chief Kelly said, "I'll call your father once we get over to the hospital, Kizzy. He can take you home once we make sure you are okay."

Clay and Mason tried to follow the police chief out of the door with Kizzy.

"Stay here," the chief told Clay and Mason. "The Captain will be here shortly to take your official statements. Afterwards, you boys are free to get on your way back to school."

Clay started to object, while holding on tightly to Kizzy's hand. "With all due respect, chief, we would like to stay with the girl until she's with her family." His voice was firm.

In an authoritative tone, Chief Kelly stated, "The girl is safe. I am personally taking responsibility for her safety and return home. You boys have done a good deed. We are all very thankful, but you need to move on with your lives. She'll be reunited with her family this afternoon." Kizzy looked up at both Clay and Mason and gave them both a big hug. Both Clay and Mason would experience their first emotional conflict as a result of caring for Kizzy.

Kizzy thought something was familiar about Police Chief Kelly, and then she remembered. He was the policeman from her school. He visited Mr. Johnson's class and talked about safety and the role of the police in the neighborhood and their role as protectors. Her teacher would always tell the kids to respect the police officers. They were there to help. Kizzy felt safe with police Chief Kelly. He was a friend of her teacher, so he was now a friend of hers.

Police Chief Kelly remembered Kizzy, too. Mr. Johnson had talked about the girl privately with him. There was a lot about the girl that was of concern and needed to be protected. "Okay boys, just wait outside for the captain. I'm sure the press will want to talk with you. Don't talk with anyone before you meet with the captain. We don't want you boys to get in any trouble," Chief Kelly said.

Clay and Mason nodded their heads. Then Chief Kelly and Kizzy left.

"I think I need to call my parents. They are going to be concerned," Mason said.

"Me too. I don't know where this is going, but we could be in a boatload of shit if they think we had anything to do with this young girl's disappearance," Clay said.

"Why did the police chief tell us not to talk with anyone until we talk with the captain? That was strange."

"Strange is not the word for it. This is bullshit. Why didn't the police chief just ask us one question, like how did we find the girl? Or why were we at the farmhouse?" Mason said.

"Do you think we're being set up? He even told us to leave if we wanted to leave," Clay said.

"Maybe just pure incompetence, sloppy work, no concerns since she's a little colored girl," Mason said as he started getting angry. "I need to call my dad!"

"Or something else," Clay said as he gestured over toward a half-blocked door. He could hear the sound of familiar voices in the background.

"Mason, does that sound like my grandpa?" Clay asked as he stood up to walk closer.

"Hey boys," a voice from the other side of the sitting room greeted them. "I'm Captain Raymond Scott. Follow me." The police station was buzzing with news that the Caldwell girl was safe. Everyone was smiling with relief. So much had happened in the city that week. The city was on edge. Tensions had been high between the officers and the town's folk.

The funeral for Kizzy's mother was just a few days away. Nobody expected the girl would ever be found alive given what she had witnessed. The hope was that her mental state was sound.

Police Chief Kelly placed three calls that afternoon. The first was to Mayor Olson, his boss, the second to Mr. Johnson, his friend and Kizzy's teacher, and the third to Hershey Hotel where Clay's grandpa was staying on a business. Mayor Olson had promised to call Mr. Caldwell to let him know his daughter was okay. He would do that after the others were contacted.

The hospital examination proved to be rather intense. They decided to sedate Kizzy to conduct some of the more invasive tests. Nothing major was discovered, although there were traces of an unusual substance in her blood and she was severely dehydrated. The plan was to keep Kizzy in the hospital a couple days to get her blood count and other organs back on track before any serious damaged occurred.

Dr. Kline was notified immediately of Kizzy's return. He rushed to the hospital to oversee her medical care. He read her test results and thought about the day she was born. How even then they knew how special she was and that her life would never be routine.

In many ways, he felt sorry for Kizzy. She would never have full control of her life. The end for her had already been mapped out. She had a great purpose to fulfill.

The world needed her abilities. He was there the day she was born and watched her from afar as she developed into this amazing little girl. He was pleased Iva and Eula made the decision to abort the attempted delivery to the Landing

Boat. His role was to ensure her safely. Was life fair? He convinced himself the answer was no. We all have a pre-determined destiny and he as well as Kiz Lamise Caldwell had theirs.

"Doctor Kline, what do you think the substance is that showing up on the tests? We are not able to identify the chemicals," a bewildered Dr. Benson asked. He stood next to Dr. Kline as the two doctors read Kizzy's results.

"Umm… I'm not quite sure. Let's run a few more tests to rule out a few things," Dr. Kline lied. He knew the experimental drug was not legal and only used in a testing lab in northern France owned by research labs controlled by Landing Enterprise.

Dr. Jay Benson said, "Okay Doc, I think that's a good idea. But how could this girl sustain the amount of drugs in her system and appear perfectly okay? Unless we are dealing with some experimental drugs not yet classified."

"Run the test, Jay. Then let's meet back here. Meanwhile let the sedation wear off and let's get some food into her system and get her hydrated. She should be fine."

Dr. Kline turned to the nurse and asked, "Did they call her family yet? We don't want anyone in this room except the medical staff until I give the order it's okay. Right now, I'm thinking three more hours will be okay for her to see her family. Let me know when they arrive. I believe it's the father, the mother is deceased."

"Yes, Dr. Kline. I'll inform the staff at the desk and others personally. Is there anything else?" Nurse Mary was a bit curious why Dr. Kline was so personally invested in this case. She recognized it was a high-profile case, yet there was something different in his tone, behavior and interest that seemed more personal, almost like this was his own child. She couldn't shake the feeling that something more was going on. She made a mental note to check into Kizzy's records when she got a chance.

Four hours later

The local TV station and radio had gotten word the girl was found and safe. Crowds began to gather at the hospital and the Caldwell home. The news was exactly what the city needed and everyone wanted to learn more about the girl's condition.

"Hello Raymond, what you are still doing here?" Dr. Kline asked.

The police chief looked at Dr. Kline and asked, "Ken, will the girl be okay? I'm as invested as you are in her safety and the safety of this city. The press is out there waiting on a statement from me. I think a joint statement might be best. Are you prepared to say how the girl is doing?"

Dr. Kline paused for a second and thought his identity would be comprised if he did the press conference with the chief. "Raymond, I think we need to get the hospital spokesperson involved with the statement about the girl – I think the hospital has its own protocol in matters such as this one."

Police Chief Raymond looked at Dr. Kline. "Yes, Yes, of course. I was just wondering if you were planning to handle this one given the particular circumstances."

"Hey chief, one of the officers at the hospital tapped on the door. Chief, we got a little disturbance down at the police station. A small crowd has gathered asking for the Chief; and oh, the mayor is on the phone. What do you want me to do?" The officer asked.

"Put the mayor through, Officer. Then go over to the station and let them know I'm on the way. I'll check in on the girl and be there soon." Police Chief Raymond promised the girl he would stay with her, and he had a demanding press outside of the hospital demanding answers. He felt trapped. But Dr. Kline was in charge, so he felt good about that. He was one of the best doctors in the country.

Dr. Kline walked across the floor and looked out of a small window. He saw the crowd gathering outside. He turned to Chief Raymond and before he could speak, Chief Raymond said, "Mayor Olson is on the way. I've briefed him on the situation, and he's already been in contact with the communications director here at the hospital. They are trying to reach you. I think the Mayor is hoping to hold a joint press conference with the hospital and the Caldwell family later this evening. Do you think that will work?"

"Should be okay," Dr. Kline replied.

The press conference was pretty routine and flat. The news confirming the girls return to Harrisburg was the headlines. The girl's condition was stated as great. The hospital planned to release her within the next two to three days. Mr. Caldwell stood next to the mayor expressionless as the mayor went into the politician mode.

Kizzy's recovery from the brief hospital stay was swift. Upon word of her pending release to her family, Clay and Mason were delighted. Their own ordeal at the police station was short and almost noneventful. They didn't want to leave Harrisburg until they knew Kizzy was safe with her family. Police Chief Raymond delivered the message himself to the boys, thanked them for their courage and told them they were free to go.

Clay and Mason left Harrisburg that night to begin their drive back to Princeton, New Jersey. They were exhausted and their weeks' vacation to talk about their life after Princeton was totally disrupted by the events of the last couple days. Both of them were ready to begin the next phase of their lives.

The silence was heartbreaking. Both Clay and Mason had so much to say to each other. Both young men could hear the voices of their parents in the echo of their consciousness, each of them hearing the same thing – Mason's parents warning Mason about the Barksdale family.

Mason's dad would say over and over again, "Mason, the Barksdale family is not your kind of people. We are not sure what's going on, but you need to move on from that family. Your heart will be broken, and they will never accept you into their family."

Mason loved Meredith Barksdale. He knew he would marry her one day. He had planned to tell Clay about Meredith before the car ran off the road near the old Barksdale Farm.

Clay was turning onto the turnpike and reaching for the radio when Mason reached over and touched his hand; trying to stop him from turning the radio on. They needed to talk.

"Man, we need to talk," Mason began. "I love you as a brother and I believe you love me the same way. I haven't been honest with you, Clay and I hope you will forgive for me. Meredith and I love each other. I know that's your baby sister and you might feel a certain way about me being with her. But Clay, you'll never have to worry about anyone loving and taking care of your sister more than me. Man, I love her." Mason continued, "Your family may never accept me, but I want you to accept me as your brother-in-law. If you can accept me, then Meredith and I will be okay. If you can't accept me, then I'll walk away and let Meredith live the life she was bought up to believe she would live. And hopefully she'll be happy with that life. But, before I do anything, I wanted to let you know where I'm coming from and I'm asking for your blessings."

Clay listened carefully to Mason. Yes, his love for him was deep. But Clay knew his family and he knew Meredith, perhaps better than Mason.

The car slowed a bit as Clay began. "My aunt Marge who lives in New York told me a story once about why she never married. Aunt Marge is one of the most beautiful, smart and fun people you will ever meet. My dad would call her his confidante. Can you imagine that brother and sister combination? My dad the businessman – strict, conservative, heartless and selfish. His sister was the complete opposite. Anyway, I asked my aunt a few years ago why she never married.

"Here's what Aunt Marge told me.

"'Clay, I had many opportunities to marry. I just never found the right combination for me at the time. You see Clay, people marry for many different reasons; some marry for love and only love. They ignore their family values or traditions. Others marry because they were bought up to select a partner who was their equal related to social class, race, economic status and religion. And others marry to offend or disappoint their family – because they come to despise the values they were taught – believing those values were wrong. If I were to find the person who made me happy, and I could love them and they loved me with no regrets for what our families thought, I would have married. You see Clay, I wanted to live my life without regrets, but I was not willing to lose everything because of love, if that was the price.'

"My aunt's words stayed with me," Clay said.

"So, what are you trying to tell me, Clay?" Mason asked, a bit confused.

"Meredith is not the one for you, Mason. She may love you, but I know my sister and if it came to losing her inherence and the life she was told she'd have, Meredith would be a very unhappy woman. You both would be miserable," Clay said.

"Did you and Meredith have a conversation about me? Sounds liked you already talked to her." Mason pressed for an answer

Watching the road and thinking about how this would hurt his friend, Clay tried to deliver the message as directly and yet as sensitively as possible.

"Mason, Meredith is dating someone else. She bought him home last month and introduced him to our parents as her fiancé. He's a resident physician at Johns Hopkins. After she introduced him to the family, she asked me to take a walk with her. That's when she told me about your relationship. I had no idea you and she were that serious until she told me. That's why I was so angry when I saw you with Meredith a few weeks ago." Clay could see the shock and hurt in Mason's face.

Mason reached over to turn the radio on and found a station playing a song that seem fitting for the moment.

The song lyrics began, "Baby, Baby, and Baby – Perhaps I loved you for all the wrong reasons. But one thing is for sure. I love you, I love you, I love you, and because I loved you, I will be a better man. I'm going to let you go. Not because I want to but because I have to. Baby, Baby, and Baby because I love, because I love. I will let you go."

Clay and Mason both started to cry. Clay had his own personal stuff. He knew he would let go of Allison. Not because he loved her. He didn't. But she loved him and needed him so much. Clay knew he would never be happy with Allison. He was looking for that love that eluded his aunt the kind of love that was complicated to the outside world and was indifferent to others as well. He could not be happy with Allison. He wanted the kind of love that spoke for itself and demanded respect because it defined the meaning of the word love.

Clay dreamed of that kind of love. His tears were tears of expectation. He had to say goodbye to Allison and find the girl in his dreams, the kind of love that made life worthwhile every day.

Mason Johnson

Mason decided to leave Princeton immediately. He did not come back for graduation. He went into the military to start his career as planned a few weeks later. He never spoke to Meredith again. And Meredith moved on with her life in a direction no one ever expected.

Meredith never spoke of Mason again, although Mason haunted her dreams and she thought of him every day for the rest of her life. She loved him, but a life with him could never be. She betrayed him and everything they dreamed possible between them had vanished from reality.

Meredith became an alcoholic, experienced three miscarriages and became addicted to pain killers. Meredith divorced her husband and shortly afterwards was committed to a mental institution. She made a big mistake. She walked away from the love of her life, Mason.

She made the biggest mistake of her life. She did what she was taught to do, but it wasn't the right thing or enough. The note she left when she committed suicide read:

"To anyone who thought they did the right thing, think hard and about who you are and what you believe. Don't be afraid to follow your heart. I was loved, so, I knew what being loved felt like, the difference between being loved and someone trying to learn to love you. Perhaps, I was lucky. I was loved twice by two very different men. I loved them both differently. You, Mason, consumed me. I didn't know how to love you. The biggest mistake of my life was letting you go. Now I how know the difference between loving and being loved.

There is nothing else left for me. Clay, Mom and Dad, I'm sorry I could never be the daughter or sister you wanted me to be. Mason, hopefully, your life is good. And you found the love of your life and you are happy. I wish with every fiber in my body that I would have been a stronger person. You Mason were in my head every day of my life. In another life, I will see you again – then I will love you in a way that has no boundary and I believe you will do the same. Until we meet again. Meredith."

After writing the letter, Meredith reached inside her purse for the gun. The metal was cold. She placed the gun against the right side of her head. Her finger hesitated for a moment and then in slow motion she pressed the trigger.

Tears fell from her eyes, her heart was beating fast, and she felt like an explosion had taken place in her head. Her body went stiff, and everything faded away. A smile was on her face when they found her.

Chapter 7

Old Friends

The phone was ringing from a distance. Jackie Steinbeck had not yet settled into her office when she received the surprise call from an old army buddy and dear friend. She was heading up her family's foundation in New York and lost the connection with many of the people she had met while a nurse in the Navy and later as a Peace Corps volunteer.

Ben Johnson was a dear friend with whom she shared many secrets and held common beliefs and hopes for the future. There was nothing she wouldn't do to thank him for saving her life when she was in the process of destroying it.

"Hello. Jackie Steinbeck. May I help you?" There was a slight pause. Ben Johnson had not called her in over eighteen years.

"Jackie, this is Ben. How are you doing?" Jackie sat up in her chair, the memories and feelings of the specialness of their friendship swept through her body when she heard the sound of his voice.

"Ben? Where the hell have you been all of these years? I've been looking for you!" Jackie was upset and glad at the same time, her emotions overflowing. She wished she could be still, cool, thoughtful. But she never could be that with him.

He smiled, feeling what he felt back then; confused and hopeful that being a closeted gay man would not take anything away from the love and desire he held for this woman. He had to run away. He knew it would only be a matter of time before she found out the truth that he was gay and would never be accepted in her family. He knew the betrayal would hurt them both. "Jackie, you sound like your old self," he chuckled. "I got your number from the Steinbeck Academy journal. I'm a teacher in Harrisburg, Pennsylvania and our library receives the journal each quarter. You were featured last year as leading the foundation there. I am calling for a favor for a student of mine. I think you may be able to help."

"Ben what do you need? Of course, I'll do what I can to help you. A teacher? Well, that's interesting. You'll have to tell me all about it." Jackie was somewhat amused to hear Ben became a teacher. She was sure he would have become a minister or even a lawyer. He was one of the smartest, compassionate, and committed individuals she had ever met.

"Jackie, would you be willing to take the train into Philadelphia to meet me at Maxie's. I want to tell you about a little girl who needs a lot of help. She's brilliant. But her story is more complicated. She needs help and I believe Steinbeck Academy for Girls is the perfect fit for her. Are you open to meet me?"

"Ben, anything you need, I'll do my best to help. I can be down on Saturday morning. Will that work for you?"

"Unfortunately, not. The girl's mother was recently killed, and I think the funeral might be this weekend. Can you meet me next week?" Ben asked.

Jackie said, "I'm not sure about next week. Give me your telephone number and I'll call you back. Would you consider coming up to the academy for a weekend? I can show you around. You'll see the changes that have been made since we were kids."

"Let me think about it Jackie. When you call back, I'll have an answer."

"Okay, Ben." Suddenly the phone went dead on the other end.

One week later

"We did it. She's in," Jackie shared with Ben as the two old friends talked on the phone. "When can you get her up here? She'll need to be here before August 2nd."

"Fantastic news, Jackie. I'll share this news with her and the school here in Harrisburg. She's a brilliant kid and her future is unlimited. You are going to love her!" Ben said.

"How is the girl? Has she been told about this possibility? Ben, this is a big step. The girl is essentially leaving home to go to boarding school for the rest of schooling. She won't be seeing much of her family. It's difficult for many of the kids to adjust to this change, especially the first year. Oh, you know that yourself having gone through six years up here," Jackie said.

"No, Jackie, we haven't told Kizzy yet about the possibility that this might happen. We didn't want to upset the girl or build up something that never happened. Her father preferred we not talk to her about it," Ben said.

"Well, Ben, it's going to happen. The early test scores and paperwork that you forwarded us suggest she is one of the brightest students to ever attend our school. We still need to interview Kiz and her father before everything is final," Jackie said.

"I think we can make that happen," Ben interrupted. "However, with all that's happened here in Harrisburg, I can't see father coming up there anytime soon. I have an idea."

"Okay, I'm open to hearing it," Jackie said.

"What if you and another member of the committee came to Harrisburg to meet Kiz and her family, spend time at her school and talk with her other teachers. You could tape record your specific session and interview with Kizzy and her father if needed or share the notes and observations from your visit with the committee after you returned to Steinbeck," Ben suggested.

"Great idea, Ben. We've actually used that approach before when a child's parent was ill, and another parent was unable to travel because of an ailing spouse. I think we can make this work.

"Do you think we can make this happen within the next couple weeks?" Jackie asked.

"I don't know. I'll talk with Mr. Caldwell later this weekend. I need to stop over the house to offer my condolences and welcome Kizzy home," Ben said.

"Sounds good. And Ben, we need to make sure the girl is mentally and physical okay after the ordeal she went through. I've been tracking as much news as I can from here. And it sounds like she's fine. But the board will need to be assured. And we'll need documentation from her doctors in Harrisburg," Jackie said.

"Let me follow up on this end and call you back on Monday. I think Ken Kline is her doctor. Do you remember him?" Ben asked.

"Ken Kline, Kline, Kline. Do you mean Dr. Kenneth Kline from Kline Research Institute?" Jackie asked with a bit of surprise. "I don't understand. Why is Ken Kline involved in the child's care?" Jackie asked.

"Jackie, there is so much you don't know about Kizzy Caldwell. When we get a chance to sit down together, I'll share more with you." Ben said.

"So, you sought me out after all these years to introduce me to this brilliant little girl. Now I'm learning that Dr. Kline is connected. Ben, you've got to share with me what's going on. Who is really behind the girl coming here?" Jackie asked with renewed interest.

"For now, let's just say, it's in all of our best interest to move this girl from Harrisburg and place her in the best environment we can to ensure she has a chance to fulfill her destiny," Ben said.

"Ben, just one question. Is she the one?" Jackie asked.

"We think so Jackie, I believe she is the one," Ben said.

Jackie leaned into the telephone, holding it tightly and no longer sitting but standing and looking out of her office window into a dense forest of trees. Holding on to hope and the ideas and teaching of the Institute that a new generation of women and men would rise, embrace new methods and approaches to systems thinking and integration, and execution that would change the world. Steinbeck Academy's role was to identify that talent early and provide them with the best educational experiences in the world. The organization recognized their mission and role was discovering this talent early and that the leader amongst this talent pool would be groomed by Steinbeck. The leader of the next generation would only be known by a few. They would know the leader by a special code given only to the birth mother.

"Ben, I'll call you tomorrow after I check with others here about what's next."

The two old friends and allies were back together on a mission they both cared about. Kiz Lamise Caldwell was a bet they would make. They were willing to give their life to ensure she was prepared to fulfill her destiny, the world's destiny.

Jackie wondered what so many in their inner circle believed, that the Kline Institute had broken the gene code enabling them to identify the missing talent trait required for future dominance. Jackie could not help but think – this little girl could be one of the seven so often predicted. Would this girl named Kiz be the leader?

The trees began to sway softly, and the moon appeared between the trees in the distance as a slight chill came over Jackie's body and the sounds of crickets chirped in the background. Unfamiliar emotions flooded her entire being. What was happening?

Jackie sat down in the chair at her desk – hands holding her head, she then thought of the note her mother wrote her during the final days of her life. She opened the drawer where she kept the note and read it out loud.

"My dearest daughter, what is destiny anyway? Only god really knows that for sure. Beware of those who say they know. Let your heart (passion), mind (abilities/talents) and body (spirit/ soul) guide you on life's journey. Be strong and stand for something outside of yourself. The different paths you take will lead to your true destiny. Oh, Jackie – don't be afraid of failure. It will happen if you take enough risks. Please do take some risks along the way. You will learn a lot about who you are. Go forward my daughter and live an amazing life. I'll laugh, cry, shout, wonder, brag, smile, clap, and bite my bottom lip, if necessary, from wherever I'm at in the universe. All in support of you. I'm here beside you right now as you read my note.

"My hope is that you'll give back unselfishly to someone else who may need your support right now. Jackie, don't over-think it. What does your heart say? Love Mom."

Jackie placed the note back in the notebook that her mom left her. She missed her so much. Her mom – the wise one!

Kizzy returns home Thursday, Afternoon May 9, 1952

"Sir, may I help you?" the receptionist asked the man standing at the desk surrounded by a bunch of kids of different ages. All of them were anxious with a mixture of excitement and expectation. Clearly, this was the family of the kidnapped girl. The receptionist followed the hospital's protocols for visitors.

"Yes, I'm Brownie Caldwell. We are here to see my daughter, Kizzy Caldwell."

The receptionist checked the directory and saw the note: "No visitors" without Dr. Kline's permission. She hesitated a moment as she found the right tone to let the family know they needed to wait until she contacted the doctor.

"Thank you, Mr. Caldwell. We have security restrictions on your daughter's floor due to the circumstances. You will need to sign in, and only the immediate family is allowed in her room. I will let them know the family is here."

Brownie Caldwell signed in and Alice and the other siblings signed in too. The other folks who came with the family, aunts, uncles, and a few members from the church, understood the restrictions and took a seat in the main lobby. The adults made small talk amongst themselves, and the kids were unusually quiet as they waited in anticipation of seeing their sister and hearing Kizzy tell her stories. They knew she would have many to tell. They also worried if she was really okay.

A tall, slim, handsome man wearing black bifocal glasses, with a folder under his arm, maybe eight or so years older than Brownie in a white doctor's jacket walked over to the family, reaching out his hand to Brownie while acknowledging the children.

"Hello, Mr. Caldwell. I'm your daughter's doctor, Dr. Kline."

"How she's doing, doctor?" Brownie asked in a direct, controlled tone.

"Well, we are very pleased with her condition and expect she can go home tomorrow. We just want to keep her here overnight for observation and few more tests," Dr. Kline said, as he and Brownie instinctively moved to a corner on the other side of the room out of hearing range from the others.

"What kind of tests," Brownie asked?

"Just some pretty routine tests, really. We did see something unusual in her blood when they bought her in. It may not be anything to worry about, but we want to run a few more test before we release her. She is terribly dehydrated, blood pressure is low, and we need to get her white cell counts back to normal. She was heavily sedated, and the residue is still in her body. Again, we are not overly concerned. She's talking, walking, and seems absolutely fine on the outside. But we do need to get the results of these additional tests before we release her and observe her overnight." Dr. Kline paused as he noticed the fatigue in Brownie's face.

"When can I see?" her Brownie asked with a little more emotion in his voice.

"If you and your family are ready now, I'll take you up. We have a private elevator over here that we'll use to get away from the press and others who I'm sure are waiting to ask you questions," Dr. Kline said.

Brownie walked over to his brothers and sisters, in-laws and church members with an update. He then returned to the family waiting room to talk with his kids.

Brownie put on a big smile as he walked across the room, and all the kids stood, not knowing what he would tell them. His smile was a clue and it helped reduce all anxiety, but the older kids knew their dad. They knew he would only bring them good news.

"Kizzy is okay, and we are going to see her in a few minutes. I just want you all to know, she's going to stay in the hospital overnight to make sure she's a hundred percent. You know Kizzy – she's doing great and wants to come home now. When you see her, she might look a little sick. That's because she has not eaten much in the last few days and the doctors need to get some water into her system. Otherwise, she's good. Are you all ready to see your sister?" Brownie asked.

The siblings smiled nervously and nodded their heads, not fully understanding what their dad was telling them, but he looked happy and that was enough for them.

Alice (the oldest) took charge as usual. "We are ready, Daddy," she said. She walked beside Brownie, and the other siblings followed and piled into the elevator.

The ride to the 7th floor seemed to take forever. Dr. Kline tried to make small talk by asking what their names and ages were. But the usually highly animated and talkative family was not in a mood for chit chat. They were thinking about Kizzy and what this reunion would be like. Finally, the elevator door opened, and Dr. Kline led them down the busy hallway toward Kizzy's room. There were nurses standing at their stations as the family passed by, the sound of an occasional monitor beeping and muffled sounds of voices as they passed patients' rooms. Some doors were half shut, and others were opened to whomever and whatever was next for them.

Brownie and Alice saw them first – the two policemen standing outside of a room at the very end of the floor. The realization of Kizzy's ordeal became even more emotional for the family. A family who would bury a loved one – a mother, wife, sister, aunt, in-law, and friend within the next twenty-four hours.

Dr. Kline stopped just a few steps before reaching Kizzy's door. "Mr. Caldwell, would you like to walk in with me first? The others can follow. We don't want to overwhelm your daughter," Dr. Kline said.

Brownie nodded and asked the kids to wait. Alice went in with him anyway.

Surrounded by windows, the room was a suite bigger than any single room in the Caldwell's family house. A sofa was on one side of the room. It could seat four people easily. A desk with a chair was anchored in the corner. A big recliner sat next to the hospital bed that looked more like somebody's king-sized bed and a small sleeping soft shape was off to the side. The room had a small kitchen with a refrigerator and a stove. The floor was covered with blue carpeting and the room was decorated in shades of beige, blues, and dark reds. A beautiful green plant sat next to the sofa near the window and a vase filled with fresh flowers sat on the cocktail table in front of the sofa. A picture of the Susquehanna River occupied the entire wall behind Kizzy's bed. The river itself could be seen flowing gently from a bay of windows, the two bridges that anchored Harrisburg and its neighboring city glistening in the sunlight of the afternoon sun. Music played softly in the background, almost missed by its softness. There she was covered in a cream and white floral comforter her head resting on a stack of white pillows.

Kizzy thought she was waking from a dream as she opened her eyes. The image of the watcher was in front of her, and she smiled. She was safe. Then, beyond the image she saw other familiar faces, her dad and sister.

Tears of joy started falling down Kizzy face. She was home. She was really safe.

Dr. Kline positioned himself off to the side.

"Daddy, Daddy," Kizzy said as she stretched her arms out to Brownie. "Daddy, daddy."

Brownie rushed to his daughter's side. Giving Kizzy one of his famous bear hugs. "My baby girl, I love you so much," Brownie whispered softly as he held his sobbing daughter in his arms. "You are home, and everything will be okay." Brownie lifted her head to look into her face. Their eyes met in the wetness of salty tears.

A nurse on duty in the room handed Brownie and Kizzy a towel.

"Well, are we ready to ask your brothers and sisters to come in?" Dr. Kline asked as he watched the father and daughter." They've been waiting to see you."

"Yes, yes," Kizzy said as Brownie moved away from her bedside to stand next to Dr. Kline and the nurse on the other side of the large room.

The door opened and Kizzy stretched her arms out for her sister and brothers. They were pleased when they saw her. She looked just like Kizzy. They had expected something different. There were lot of giggles, more kisses and tears, all the kids were happy to see Kizzy, and they couldn't wait until she was back home to tell them what happened. The kids were already told not to ask Kizzy about the kidnapping or tell her she would not be coming home with them until after her mother's funeral.

Dr. Kline stood in the corner and watched as did the nurse, and the two policemen stood outside the door that was now open.

Fifteen minutes had passed before Dr. Kline looked over toward Brownie. The two men had decided to keep the visit with the kids short. They would tell Kizzy together with Alice there. They knew Kizzy would be disappointed not to be going home with them, and she would later be disappointed to know that she missed her mother's funeral. Alice would help them get Kizzy to understand everything was okay.

"Okay, we need to clear the room and talk with Kizzy. Mr. Caldwell, you and your daughter Alice are staying right?" Dr. Kline asked.

After the room was cleared, the news was given to Kizzy. Alice had brought with her a small suitcase with Kizzy's going home clothes. She unpacked the suitcase for Kizzy to see as the doctor explained why she would be staying a little while longer. Alice pulled out Kizzy's favorite dress – a yellow and black polka dot dress, white socks and black shoes. Alice hung the dress in the closet in the room for Kizzy to see. Kizzy had no negative reaction to the news that she had to stay in the hospital overnight. She felt safe and knew she would be headed home soon.

It had been a glorious afternoon for the Caldwell family, a moment of happiness in the midst of a pending funeral for Emily Caldwell the next day. The emotional roller coaster for the family was overwhelming, but the family was proving to be strong, the attributes that both Landing Enterprise and Shadow Corporation expected from the little girl they both were invested in acquiring for their own interest one day. Dr. Kline was even more confident than ever that little Kizzy Caldwell was one of the chosen eight. Whether or not she was the leader was too soon to know.

Outside the hospital

The crowd was still gathered outside of the hospital, and it appeared to have grown larger and more joyous, as word of the girl's safety had spread throughout the community. The local radio station truck was parked across the street from the hospital entrance and the local reporters were visible by the shirts they wore. The diverse crowd cheered and clapped when they saw the family leave the hospital. There were questions, lots of questions about what happened to the little girl. There were major concerns due to the racial tensions across the country. The thoughts of the corpses earlier that week at the school and Emily Caldwell's murder hung heavy over the small town and negro communities. Kizzy coming home was good news, but everyone sensed they needed to protect the little girl.

"Kizzy what are you looking at?" Alice asked in a low whisper.

"My secret friend. I was saying thank you," Kizzy whispered in Alice's ear.

Alice gave Kizzy a big hug. She was thinking about Kizzy's imagination and how she made things up. Alice was worried about Kizzy and if she would ever tell the truth about what happened to her. The police had told their father to ask the family not to ask Kizzy about what happened until they gave the okay. So, no family member asked her what happened the day she disappeared or knew what she told the police. What the family knew was that two college boys found her in an old farmhouse in Hershey; she was alone and appeared drugged.

The ride home was filled with laugher and multiple conversations, the siblings all talking at once. Brownie Caldwell was driving his new Buick and an old friend on the other side in the passenger seat, Rev. Dinkins.

Richard Dinkins had hurried to the Caldwell house once he got word the girl had been found. He had a lot on his mind. Marylee's possible role in Kizzy's disappearance, the break-up of his marriage, his kids' future and the funeral for Emily Caldwell. He needed to talk with Brownie about what was going on… but now was not the time. His friend had so much happening in his own life. He couldn't place anything more on Brownie's heart.

"Hey Richard, you are pretty quiet over there. Are you okay?"

"I'm okay. Just thinking about all that's happened this past week, how God has blessed us with the coming home of Kizzy. And I was thinking about tomorrow and the service for Emily."

"Is that all?" Brownie probed as he pulled the car in front of the house.

Richard Dinkins never got a chance to respond. The excitement and noise from the kids to be home engulfed the car as the doors flew open and the kids stumbled out of the car… headed for the front door.

"Come on Kizzy!" Carmen yelled, "you are home." Kizzy's brother grabbed her hand to help her up the steps.

Mr. Caldwell walked closely behind her as the older kids pushed against the old door and entered the house.

Old Pal was welcoming her home with his barking. She recognized his bark but could not respond. Off to the corner she saw a shadow approaching from near the alley next to their house. It was the Watcher. Then she felt his hands gently on her shoulders, as if lifting her up the stairs, over the view and memories of her mother's bloody body next to hers and the image of her mother's limp head cradled in her lap. No one knew the depth of pain she felt except the Watcher.

Kizzy began to hum her special song: "Wake me in the morning, afternoon, or night- anytime to let me you are here. I need you. I need you and I want you near. Can you hear my cry can you hear my cry. Please let me know you still care. Do I dare tell a soul you love me? Wake me when you are here." Kizzy repeated the song in a low tone. No could really understand what she was mumbling to herself.

The Funeral – Saturday, May 10, 1952

The younger Caldwell children did not attend their mother's funeral. Instead, they remained home with neighbors and community leaders who volunteered to help the family with meals and welcome mourners after the service.

Brownie Caldwell didn't want the younger kids exposed to such grief. He wanted them to remember their mother the way she was. He sat on the front row with his daughter Alice and oldest son Larry. Emily's siblings and other relatives were there too. The golden-brown casket positioned in front of him was closed. A picture taken a few years earlier stood next to her coffin, and flowers were beautifully arranged around her, and a family spray of roses lay on top of the closed coffin. The service was simple. Brownie knew Emily would not want much of fuss. But given the fact she was murdered, people were there from all over the city and county, people who did not know the family but were there to show their support and respect.

"Will you forgive? Can you forgive?" Rev. Richard Dinkins said as he closed his sermon to end the funeral. Rev. Dinkins spoke those words with so much emotion and sincerity that those who knew him best wondered if the message was about Emily Caldwell murder and to the community or was there a deeper meaning – something more personal. After all, Marylee Dinkins was not at the service, and she had been linked to Caldwell girl's disappearance.

Brownie listened to his old friend's words and heard something disturbing in his voice; a broken man's urgent plea for help. Brownie stood in the procession before they headed to the ceremony to bury Emily in her final resting place.

Brownie thought he had to hold it together for the rest of the family, his suit jacket was moist from the sobbing faces nestled on his shoulders and chest, his heart beating fast from the pain that rested there from so many who embraced him and laid their grief on top of his own. He was tired and feeling weak.

Tears ran uncontrollably down Brownie's face. A stranger walked up to him and instead of another embrace, the stranger gently wiped his tears away. Brownie felt so comforted in the stranger's presence and tried to look more closely at the blurred image in front of him.

In a low voice the stranger said, "you and your family will be alright. Give Kizzy the book above the kitchen ceiling and let her go. Forgive Richard."

"What happened?" Brownie asked as his sister and Richard were standing over him and a few others were fanning him.

"You fainted," said Richard Dinkins right after Emily's coffin was lowered in the ground. "We were just getting ready to send someone to call an ambulance. Are you okay? How do you feel? You've been out for a while."

"I'm okay," Brownie said. He looked around for the stranger, then realized he must have experienced the stranger while he had fainted.

"Okay. You've had a tough week are you sure you don't want to go to the hospital and get checked-out," Richard continued.

"No, no, I'm good." Brownie stood up and looked at the concerned faces of his oldest kids who had just lost their mother. They had to be afraid seeing him fall.

"Okay gang, let's go home," Brownie said with his booming voice and reassuring smile.

Alice and Larry gathered around their dad and gave him a big hug. They walked across the grass away from their mother's grave with their heads held high, hands clasped together, in a line of solidarity and confidence.

Richard Dinkins looked and thought. The Caldwell family will be okay. The love they had for each other was deep and Emily and Brownie Caldwell were good people. If any family could weather the tragedies and heartaches, it was the Caldwell family.

Cars were doubled parked along the narrow street as the family returned from Emily Caldwell's funeral. People were entering and exiting the small house at a steady pace. Flowers had been placed on part of sidewalk and on the steps of the store next door. The weather was beautiful, and the late afternoon air gave promise for a refreshing ending to a stressful day.

"Kizzy, Kizzy," Alice yelled as she pointed to the window where she knew her little sister would be. "We are home."

Brownie and the rest of the family continued walking up the steps as they waved to the little girl sitting on the windowsill.

Kizzy waved backed as she joyously jumped to the floor and ran down the steps to join the rest of the family. She was glad to be home, while understanding the sadness of the moment. The hospital did not want to release her, but Brownie's insistence she would be okay at home. He promised to bring her back for a checkup on Monday morning.

People were everywhere. They were gathered at the house to eat after saying good-bye to her mom. Kizzy saw so many familiar faces, and many of them were staring directly at her.

One woman approached Kizzy. "You poor child, are you okay?" The woman asked.

The collective voices of the women from church. They gave her no breathing space or room to respond before a bunch of other questions rattled from their tongue.

Another woman approached. "Baby girl baby you look like you need something to eat, did you get any food? Come on let me get you something to eat," the woman said as she reached for Kizzy's hand.

Yet another woman reached to grab Kizzy. "Oh, child let me give you a hug," the sobbing woman said as she continued to reach for Kizzy.

The attention was overwhelming, and Kizzy tried to move away as the women from the church were pushing and pulling her toward the food table while others stared and whispered in corners about her ordeal.

Kizzy wanted to scream. She felt faint as if she had no energy. She wanted to run back up the steps to her room. She thought, please God help me.

Brownie Caldwell could see the connotation as he walked toward his daughter.

"Oh Brownie, I'm so sorry," the woman holding Kizzy hand yelled out as she tried to embrace Kizzy's father. "Oh, you poor dear. If there is anything I can do for you and your family, please let me know."

"Thank you, Fannie. We'll be okay. Why don't you join the others and get something to eat," Brownie said as he took Kizzy's hand and pulled his daughter next to him.

Fannie looked a bit upset that she was so abruptly dismissed, and the girl was removed from her clutch. She bent over and gave the girl a kiss and tried to whisper something in her ear. Kizzy turned her head and smuggled closer to her dad.

Brownie walked with his daughter toward the front of the room, allowing her to spend time with the rest of her siblings. He finally sat down. Lost in his own thoughts during this rare moment of privacy, Brownie started to think about what he was going to do with six kids and no wife. He just knew he had to put a plan in place to give them the best shot in life he could.

Someone was talking to him.

"May I sit down here with you?" The familiar voice was his friend Richard Dinkins.

Brownie looked up as Richard handed him a glass of water.

"Thank you, man," Brownie said as he moved over to make room for Richard on the old sofa.

Both men laughed as the sofa sank to the floor under the weight of the two large men.

"How are you holding up?" Richard asked.

"I'm worried, Richard. I'm worried about my kids. They desire to have both a mother and father. But if anybody should be here with them it should Emily. She deserved more," Brownie said.

"We'll find out who did this Brownie. I'm with you as long as it takes. And man, you are an excellent father. God has a plan. You will not be forsaken. Trust him," Richard said.

Suddenly, the men were interrupted by a man calling Brownie's name.

"Brownie Caldwell, do you remember me?" The man asked.

Brownie and Richard both tried to get up from the sofa at the same time, both men falling backwards on the sofa and struggling again to get up. Everyone in the room who saw the event just burst out laughing, a comedy in the making watching those two big men trying to get off that sofa together, trying not to touch each other and spilling the water they were holding all over each other. They laughed so hard at the other that they were actually crying. Just what Browne needed?

The kids came running in the room to see what was going on and everybody joined in the much-needed laughter.

"Okay folks, the comedy show is over," Brownie said as he regained his composure and helped Richard stand.

Brownie walked over to the man and immediately recognized him, although he did not know the woman with him.

"Mr. Silverman, thanks you for coming and forgive the comedy scene," Brownie said.

"Oh, no problem. Actually, I was delighted to see you have some fun. I can't imagine how difficult it must be for you to lose Emily. By the way, the service was beautiful, absolutely beautiful. Anyway, I need a few moments in private with you. I think this is something you may want to know as soon as possible," Mr. Silverman continued with a smile. The woman stood next to him with a briefcase.

"Well, the only private place in the entire house right now is upstairs in one of the bedrooms." Brownie turned to the female with Mr. Silverman and asked, "Miss, are you okay with the upstairs arrangement?"

"Mr. Caldwell, my name is Vanessa Marshall. Thank you for asking. Yes, that will be just fine. I'm an attorney at the Bridgewater Law Firm in Milledgeville Georgia."

"Okay, I'll lead the way. Before we go up would either of you like some water or something to eat?" Brownie asked.

"Yes, I'll have a cup of that coffee that I smell and a piece of that pound cake over there," Mr. Silverman said as he made his way to the dessert table.

"Ms. Marshall, would you like anything?" Brownie asked.

"Nothing, I'm okay," Vanessa Marshall said as she smiled at Brownie.

Brownie led the way after Mr. Silverman finished his dessert and grabbed a cup of coffee.

The room upstairs was just as Emily had left it. Brownie was unable to sleep there; he had moved to the basement where his workshop with an old bed had been established. So, he knew the room would be presentable. There were two chairs in the room. He would sit on the bed and give his guest the chairs. Emily's vanity could serve as a desk as well as the nightstand.

"Let me turn on the light for you folks," Brownie said as he reached over Vanessa Marshall. The smell of her perfume caught him a bit off guard. And he felt guilty to have a sense of pleasure on the very day he had buried his wife.

"Now, is that better?" Brownie asked as he turned on the lamp.

"Thank you, Mr. Caldwell," Vanessa said as she sheepishly looked at him and thought, what a beautiful man.

"Well, what's this all about, Ben?" Brownie asked, looking at Ben Silverman who seemed occupied organized papers in front of him.

Brownie Caldwell realized how special Kizzy was and he would do anything to protect her and the rest of his family. After reading the journal his wife had left for him, he knew what he needed to do.

Kiz would head off to boarding school and her life would be different. She maintained a close bond with Carmen and Vincent. Alice was the oldest and she was graduating soon. She would be okay. She was smart and independent. Already, she was talking about staying with relatives in New York, taking a job at IBM were her cousin worked; later she would become a successful corporate executive, although her personal life was a disaster. Carmen was still in high school – but she worked part-time at the local hospital. She wanted to go to college in Washington, D.C. – Howard University. Later she would become a doctor. Carmen was determined, smart as a whip and the most compassionate of all of his kids. Brownie never worried about Carmen; he always felt she would be on the side of what was right. Other than Kizzy, the three boys worried him the most. Perhaps because they were black boys; Larry and Leon had decided in high school that careers in the military were their paths. Both would become officers. Larry would be killed in Vietnam right after making Captain. Leon's career was exemplary; becoming a Colonel in the Army, he settled in Washington, D.C. where Carmen lived. He never married; it was rumored he was secretly in love with his brother's (Larry's) wife... when she remarried. The rumor continued that it broke his heart; he remained close friends with his sister-in-law, a sad situation for both of them.

Vincent, the youngest of the boys and the most gifted athletically would go on to play football at the University of Michigan and later a distinguished all pro football Hall of Fame career with the Pittsburgh Steelers, returning to his hometown as a successful entrepreneur and community leader.

Somehow Brownie knew his kids would be okay.

Chapter 8

The Journal

1955

Three years had passed since Emily's murder. The police had no leads, and interest in the case had faded. Brownie sat in the kitchen alone thinking about his wife and finally getting the energy to go through her private belongings. He looked at the light blue box that had been tucked on the top shelf closet behind Emily's hat boxes in their bedroom. He had given the hats away to his sister Kara a year ago. She promised to take care of them, knowing how much Emily enjoyed wearing the hats to church. Brownie had given Emily's other clothes to Kara almost immediately after the funeral. He decided to keep the few pieces of jewelry Emily had for his daughters.

Emily's hats were a little more difficult for him to let go. There was something about the hats that he had trouble giving away. Finally, he was able to let them go too. Still, there remained the little blue box that was tied up with black shoestrings sitting on the shelf.

Brownie poured himself another cup of coffee and decided to go upstairs and get the box. It was time to open it and then move on. It was just that Emily protected, actually hid, that box, though he knew it was there.

As he walked up the steps, he thought some more about Emily. He would see her occasionally moving her hat boxes around and taking that box with her to the kitchen at night while she was writing. He assumed whatever she was writing was in the box.

The box was really light, but he knew something was inside. He took it downstairs, sitting at the kitchen table where he began to untie the strings and inside, he saw a stack of letters. As he flipped through, he saw they were addressed to him, each of his kids, his sister Kara, Marylee Landrieu Dinkins, and Dr. Kline.

Brownie was wondering why Emily would write letters to Marylee and Dr. Kline. Nothing else was in it except stationary envelopes, two pens, and a pencil.

Brownie placed the letter addressed to him on the table and put the other letters back inside the box. He was beginning to feel sad and doubted whether or not he was ready to read the letter from Emily. For some reason he just could not open the letter.

"Good morning, Dad, what are you doing?" Alice asked as she came into the kitchen.

"Oh, just going through a box of your mom's stuff that was still in the bedroom."

Alice opened the refrigerator, taking out some eggs, bacon, and sausage.

"Well, I'm going to get breakfast started before the rest of the gang comes running downstairs," Alice said. She took the skillets out and the biscuit pan and began to get breakfast started.

"I'll put the grits on while you do that," Brownie offered.

"No, Dad, I got this. You go ahead and do what you were doing. I'm good."

"Alice, okay, but you need to learn how to accept help. I hope you learn how to say 'yes, I could use a hand or just thank you I would like that.' I don't want you to grow up thinking your role is to cook while the men in your life sit and watch. You find something for the boys and men to do; or else we'll expect you to do everything." Brownie continued, "Alice, even if you have to make something up. Don't let people take advantage of you, especially men. Do you understand what I'm trying to tell you?"

"Daddy, I don't know why you are always lecturing me. If you want to help, why don't you go ahead and do something. Why do I have to tell you what to do? If you really want to do it, just do it," Alice said.

"I see you really don't get it. I wish your mom was here. Maybe hearing it from a woman would make a lot more sense."

"Daddy, why don't you peel the potatoes, if you want something to do? I thought you were busy with whatever you were looking at inside that box," Alice said. "And, Dad, the onions and green peppers need chopping too!" Alice continued.

"Ok, ok, ok, that's what I'm talking about, Alice."

They both start laughing as Carmen walked in the kitchen.

"What are you two laughing about?" Carmen said as she leaned in to give her dad a kiss on the cheek. "Good morning!"

"Good morning sweetie. Hey, I going to get up from here and leave you too young beautiful girls and great cooks to work your magic in this kitchen…. I'm just in the way," Brownie said as he picked up the box and pushed the chair under the table.

"Oh no, not so quick mister. We need your magic to fix those fried potatoes," a laughing Carmen continued. "Dad, you make the best home fried potatoes in the world."

"Carmen, flattery will get you everything," Brownie said as he stood up. "Girls, I tell you what. I'll teach you how to make my secret potatoes if you cut up the onion, potatoes, and green peppers. I need to run upstairs and put this box away and get your brothers out of bed. I'll be back down to cook the potatoes and share my secret ingredients with you. Do we have a deal?"

Carmen spoke first. "Okay, that sounds reasonable." Alice nodded in agreement as she took the box of grits from the cupboard.

"I'll peel the onions and cut the peppers. Everything will be here waiting for you, Daddy," Carmen said.

"Okay Carmen," Brownie said, laughing "you got me. Look like your mom taught you well. See what I mean, Alice, sometimes you just got to ask for support and accept it even when you don't think you need it or get everything you ask for. Doesn't make you any stronger or weaker, just place more value on you as a person." Brownie left the kitchen to return the box to the bedroom.

"Is Dad lecturing you again, Alice?"

"Sigh … yeah. I don't know why. Since mom died, he's been on my case every day about something. Seems like he's judging who I am and trying to make me into someone I'm not," Alice said.

"Well, if you want my two cents or not, I'm going to give it to you anyway. Dad's right. I think what he's trying to tell you is to stand up for yourself. People will respect you more if you don't let them run all over you. Alice, people use you. You do too much for everybody and nothing for yourself. You don't even have a boyfriend. You are so worried about Dad. Making Dad happy. Alice it's not your job to be our mom or Dad's wife. Everybody sees what's happening. You need to move on with your life. You'll be graduating in a few weeks, and you already have a job. If I were you, I'd been trying to get out of here."

Alice turned to look at Carmen, thinking Carmen was always outspoken, independent and took more risks than she did. And it seems her parents always gave her more freedom and talked to her differently. It was more like a conversation.

"Well, I guess it could be worse," Alice said as she poured water into the pot for the grits. "Dad is extremely tough on Leon, Larry and Vincent. He drills them every day about school, their friends, how they spend their free time, news of the day, their future. I mean he's in their face all the time about something. So, it could be worse for me," Alice said.

"Come on Alice, Dad loves us all. He just tries to make men out of Vincent, Leon and Larry. I think letting Kizzy go off to boarding school broke his heart. He tries to do what's best for us," Carmen said.

"Why are you so reasonable about things related to Dad and his actions and such a bitch about everything else?" Alice said.

"Oh, here we go, you calling me names now… hey. I don't need this. You do whatever you need to do Alice. I'm going back upstairs. And, by the way, nobody wants to eat your nasty cooking anyway. You can't cook!" Carmen yelled as she left the kitchen, passing her dad on the way.

"Hey, hey what's going on in here?" Brownie asked as he passed Carmen on the steps.

"Nothing, Dad, I just told Alice the truth. She can't cook!" Carmen said as she tried to move past her dad to the steps.

"Wait a minute, young lady. You don't run this house. I do! Now get back in that kitchen. Did you peel the potatoes like I told you?"

"No, Alice made me mad," Carmen said in a defiant tone.

The two of them walked the kitchen. Alice was standing next to the stove staring at both of them while she held a knife in one hand and potatoes in the other.

Both Carmen and Brownie looked at her. She looked stone crazy!

They were both staring and then burst out laughing, and Alice joined them.

"Girls, I'm going to share my secret recipes and the timeline for which dishes to prepare first. Carmen, go get me an apron. Alice, come over here and watch closely as I make this potato casserole. Turn the boiled grits off. I'm going to share another recipe with you girls today." Almost like magic, the girls became their dad's assistant in the kitchen that morning. They had never seen him take control like that. He would always tell them how to fix something or how to improve a dish, but to show them how was different. They worked together that morning to fix their best breakfast since their mom died, three years ago.

"Wow, this is the best breakfast in a long time," Leon said as he ate the egg and grits dishes.

"Yeah, these sausages are my favorite," echoed Larry.

"And I love the biscuits," Vincent said as he bit into his third butter and jelly-filled Pillsbury biscuit.

"Alice, you did your thing," Leon voiced as he scooped another mouthful of grits and eggs into his mouth. "Uhmm-mmm, this is good." Everybody nodded in agreement with their mouths full.

Brownie looked at his girls and winked, then said, "Alice, your cooking taste just as good as your momma's – delicious."

Carmen smiled, realizing her dad was building-up Alice's confidence and said, "Alice you'll have to make these potatoes again next Saturday. I think they are better than Dad's." Everyone laughed and nodded their heads in agreement.

Alice didn't know what to say, so she stood up and started taking the empty bowls off the table. She felt uncomfortable taking credit for something that was not true. She helped, but her dad did the real cooking. Did they all know the truth and were just going alone with their dad?

"Sit down Alice. You've done enough this morning and we're thankful. The boys will clean up the kitchen today. New rule!" Brownie said as Vincent, Leon and Larry begin to protest out loud together.

"No Dad, I can clean up. Let me do it. Vincent has a football game today and Leon and Larry have something planned too. I can do it," Alice said.

Brownie just looked at his daughter and wondered if he was the one to teach her and help build her confidence or was he going about this all wrong?

"I'll help you Alice," Carmen volunteered as she began to remove dishes from the table.

"Vincent, you can help with the trash before you leave, Leon and Larry, one you come here and sweep up and one of you mop the kitchen after the girls finish. Boys, meanwhile, go clean your room and make sure your bathroom is cleaned," Brownie barked in frustration.

Everyone scattered off to do their tasks. Brownie began to think of their mother, asking himself, what would she do? Was his decision to send Kizzy off to boarding school all the way in Boston the right decision? He missed her too. Three years had passed since she went to Boston. She had only been home four times in the two years (during the Thanksgiving and Christmas holidays). He could already see in his baby girl. She was seven when he agreed to let her go; she was ten now and was not able to come home to celebrate her birthday. The kids all signed a card and sent it to her instead. He had not heard from Kizzy in a few weeks. That was unusual. She would write to him and the family at least once a week. The letters were now less frequent.

While the kids were off doing their tasks, Brownie decided to read the letter Emily had left for him in the blue box. He walked upstairs and closed their bedroom door, took the letter from the box and sat on the bed, opened the letter and began to read.

Dear Brownie,

Do you remember my grandma Mammie who worked at Graceland & Glory Paper Mill when we were kids? Well, anyway, Grandma always encouraged me to write. She would say write it down, so you won't forget, don't let somebody else tell your story or steal your thoughts, write it down. When I was fifteen, I started to keep a journal. Grandma would bring me scraps of paper from the mill and told me to write. She would tell me stories about other slaves. One of the stories was about a slave girl name Genevieve. She worked at a planta-tion in Louisiana. Grandma knew the story because my grandmother's sister lived on that plantation before coming to Georgia where I was raised as you already know. Anyway, the woman named Genevieve practiced witchcraft, as did my great aunt. Genevieve was said to have placed a curse on the plantation owners and her family. Anyway, my aunt and other family members found out about the curse. My grandmother's sister Lucy was thought to be an original spirit an angel who from time to time would interfere in the affairs of other slaves and people. She was actually very spiritual and believed in things from other worlds in the old testament. She was both feared and loved. It was said Genevieve, who many believed was possessed, feared Lucy the most; and somehow knew that her own redemption and elevation to a higher level in the spirt and witchcraft world was through Lucy and her sister, Ma Hattie. Lucy refused to offer redemption or help Genevieve – but there was one catch. The only way Genevieve or any of her descendants could be free of the demonic curse was through a descendant of Aunt Lucy's who would be born in the 1940s. This brings me to Kizzy.

Stay with me Brownie …. I know this sounds crazy.

Brownie couldn't believe what he was reading. He got off the bed and walked over to the window and looked out at nothing in particular, just looking. He could hear the boys in their room cleaning up and arguing with each other. He had no idea what else Emily wanted to tell him. Still holding the letter, he sat down in the chair next to the window. It was almost 9:30 a.m. and he promise Richard that he would meet him at the church at 10 a.m. to help with some repairs. But he had to read more before leaving.

Do you remember that day when we were coming from school? I think it was 1934. I was fifteen years old at the time. I think you were 19, and I veered off the walking path with you and the other kids from school? Remember when you, Bobby Smith, Francis Banks, Gene Macklin and Lillian Harris found me unconscious on the old country road? I asked you did you see the old woman on the road. You all said no and that I was hallucinating because I hit my head. Well, I don't know if you remember that far back – anyway, I never told anybody what the old woman told me that day. It was about Kizzy and her destiny.

I've known since Kizzy was born that she was not mine. Of course, I gave birth to her, but she is the daughter of the universe. Sounds crazy, right? Well, it's true. My death was a sacrifice to ensure Kizzy fulfills her mission.

Brownie, I need you to do 3 things for me: 1) in the kitchen behind the broom closet is book journal wrapped in a brown paper bag. I need you to give that to Kizzy when she turns 15 years old. I don't think I will be living that long. 2) Give each of my children the letter addressed to them – Brownie- don't read their letters

*and 3) Brownie, fall in love again – you are a good man
and deserve to be loved. And Brownie please forgive and
trust Richard.*

Love Emily,

The sound of a car horn was blowing from outside
and Larry's voice and knock on the bedroom door bought
Brownie back to reality.

"Dad, Rev. Dinkins is waiting for you outside. Do you
want me to tell him you are on the way?" Larry asked.

"That's okay Larry, I am ready, and I'm going down now."
Brownie put the letter back in the box and pushed the box
under the bed. He walked out of that room a confused man.

When he reached the front door, he decided to holler
back at the kids. "Okay, I'll be going down to the church
for a few hours. I'll be back by 12:30pm. Larry and Leon,
make sure Vincent's ready. He has a game at 4:00pm. He
needs to be at school by 1:30pm. We can all go down the
school together. Carmen and Alice; your Aunt Kara wants
you over her house by 1:00pm. Be ready when I get back!
Okay gang, we'll all leave together at 1:00pm. I'll see you
in a few hours." Brownie left the house, still thinking about
what he had just read.

"Are you ready to go do some work for the Lord?" Richard
asked as Brownie got into the car. Brownie was silent as the
men drove the short distance to the church.

The church was under major repairs due to expansion, and several men had volunteered to help out on this Saturday morning, so Richard and Brownie didn't have much time to talk.

Richard had become accustomed to the periods of silence between the two men. He didn't give Brownie's mood any thought. He too had lost a wife and so he understood the responsibilities of raising kids as a single father, although he did have a lady friend in his life.

The day moved on as planned. The evening was more difficult for Brownie.

Around 10:00 p.m. when the kids were all in bed, Brownie decided to take a short walk to the neighborhood bar. He was still shaken and confused by what he had read in Emily's letter and just needed to get away from the house for a while and have a drink.

Most of the folks in the bar were from the neighborhood, a few from the church, and a surprising number of patrons who were regulars lived on the other side of town where all the yuppie black folks lived. Brownie took a seat at the far end of the bar, clearly signaling 'don't bother me please!' But it was a Saturday night, and the bar was full, the music loud and people were having a good time.

"Hey Brownie, good to see you man. I haven't seen you in a while. How are you doing man? Your kids, how are they doing? Wow, I haven't seen you in here, well, since your wife passed away," Scotty the bartender said as he leaned over to shake Brownie's hand.

"I'm okay Scotty. How you doing, man? You still dating Connie Walker?" Brownie asked with a smirk.

"Oh man, that's old news. Connie got married to some guy from D.C. and moved there last year. Man, she broke my heart, and probably ten other guys'," Scotty said with a laugh. "What can I get you man? Still drinking Jack Daniels on the rocks?"

Brownie nodded his head affirming the order. "Yep – you got it."

"How you doing?" Brownie said to the stranger sitting next to him. The man who staring into his untouched drink! The stranger didn't say a word just kept staring into the glass.

"He's been like that for the last ten or fifteen minutes," Scotty whispered to Brownie. "I figure, man got some problems and need to be left alone."

The stranger turned to Brownie… his eyes were dark, his face contorted. He wore a hat, so you couldn't see much, and his coat was oversized, yet he didn't look like a beggar – just a man with deep issues.

"My name is Victor. Man, I haven't slept in weeks. I keep having these dreams about a young girl with extraordinary gifts who will change the world. Some scary stuff man. Some messed-up people in the world." Victor picked-up his glass and finished the drink. He turned to Brownie and said, "Good luck man," then left the bar.

Brownie was shaken and confused by the stranger's comments.

Chapter 9

Recall

1976

Kiz was pleased that Colin had suggested they meet in New York. The train from Boston to New York was a much easier commute for her and she loved the idea of spending a weekend in New York. The two women had agreed to meet at the newly renovated Tavern on the Green near Central Park.

Colin arrived just a few minutes before Kiz, and a hostess was leading Colin to a table facing Central Park when Kiz entered the restaurant and saw Colin. Colin turned to sit, when she saw her old friend. The two women embraced tightly without speaking- when they did let go, both of them sat down focusing intensely on the other for a few seconds.

Colin began the conversation. "Kizzy I can't believe we are finally together. You look great! Wow, it's been a long time! The last time we were together, we were sixteen years old. I'm so glad you accepted my invitation to meet."

"I'm glad to be here. But where do we even begin?" Kiz asked with a laugh, "Colin, you look exactly the same as you did that day you told me you were leaving Steinbeck. How are you doing, and why now?"

"Did you know my brother Kyle was severely wounded in Vietnam and had to retire from the Military?" Colin asked with a more serious tone.

"No, I didn't know that." Kiz paused, then she smiled and continued, "I remembered that day my sister Carmen ran into the house from the candy store across from our house. We lived on Cumberland Street then. Carmen had just met your brother Kyle. I must have been seven or eight years old. I remembered that day so clearly. My dad was so angry with Carmen because she was so excited about meeting this new boy. Later I learned the boy my sister was so crazy about was your brother, Kyle. None of kids understood why dad was so upset with Carmen every time she would mention Kyle's name." Kiz said.

She continued, "Our mom would say, 'one day you'll understand why your dad is so angry. Just live long enough – you'll experience and see things to help you understand. Colin, my dad was afraid Carmen would get her heart broken. Carmen falling in love with a white boy was not what my dad had in mind for any of his girls. Interesting, I forgot about Carmen and Kyle when my mom died. How is your brother doing?" Kiz asked.

Colin motioned for the waitress to come over. She turned toward Kiz and said, "My brother Kyle died ten years ago.

Carmen was with him when he died. She was his doctor at the VA hospital in Virginia, where he asked to spend his last days," Colin said.

"I'm so sorry Colin, I just didn't know," Kiz said as she reached across the table to touch Colin's hand.

The old friends just held each other's hand tightly for a moment, and in that moment, they were flooded with memories and emotions that had complicated both of their relationship and life.

"You know Kiz, I think Carmen and Kyle fell in love as teenagers, but society taught them it was wrong for them to be together; even though they both married other people, you could sense the attraction between them never left. I remembered my dad always telling Kyle, life is not fair. Some things are just not meant to be. Mom would tell him to be happy. When we visited my grandfather, I would overhear my grandfather and Kyle talking about the future. Grandpop told Kyle to be happy and live his own life, not my father's. The two of them would talk about my grandfather's company and projects he was working on. Kyle loved those conversations."

Colin looked out of window and paused before continuing, "too bad Carmen and Kyle never got a chance. My brother died with your sister, my mom and dad standing by his side. Kyle's wife didn't get to the hospital before Kyle died. Mom told me later that he reached out for your sister's hand, held it while he summoned my mom and dad and her closer to him. He smiled at all three of them and then whispered 'I love you'; then he took his last breath. His eyes were focused on your sister. Mom believed he meant for all of them to know he always loved Carmen."

"Colin, I didn't know. I'm so sorry. My sister never said anything. She actually broke up with her husband about ten years ago. She never gave a reason for their break-up. And she was always so sad. Now I know why," Kiz said.

Kiz continued, "Do you remember the incident that happened when we were in grade school?"

Colin nodded, shifting a bit in her chair and quietly said, "Kiz, are you talking about the burned corpses who spoke your name, the incident in the park after we stole my dad's gun or when you arrived at Steinbeck and they tried to separate us? Oh, and not to mention the Barksdale's," Colin said.

Kiz turned to look out the window, then she looked at her childhood friend, thinking about the many secrets they shared and said, "Colin, tell me about your uncle's connection with – Landing Enterprise."

"Unfortunately, I don't know much. My mother tried really hard to separate us from my uncle's family. My dad barely talked about his brothers when we were young. As we got older, my brothers became interested in the family business and went to work for my uncles." Colin continued, "My uncles were widely admired by their family, although I always stayed away from their business. I guess I was always on my mom's side. So, there's not much I can share, Kiz.

"Hey, what's with all these questions about my family? I haven't seen you in fifteen years! I think you and I have a lot of other things to catch-up on and discuss."

Kiz nodded in agreement as the waitress came over to their table and took their order.

After an hour of small talk and catching-up on their family, politics, and their current life, the conversation drifted to the time they spent the most time together, grade school.

"Whatever happened to our teacher who was a retired military officer? Mr. Johnson? He was so protective of us as kids. Did you call me because of what happened that day in grade school, Kiz?"

"Yes, Colin we've never talked about that day. Do you remember the burned corpses and what you told me about the men at your father's house the day before the incident at school?"

Colin sat straight up in her chair, took a deep breath and a sip of her water, and as she placed the glass down, she leaned forward and bit her bottom lip and glanced out to the window. Her eyes were dark, deep in the mystery of another place. She was almost dazed. It seemed like forever before she answered Kiz's question. In reality it was only seconds.

"The nightmares from that day and the day before have never gone away. Kiz, even though I was a kid, I had the responsibility to tell an adult what I knew. I told only you. You were a kid too. Through the years, as I've gotten older, my understanding of what I overheard and the significance of it has cause me to separate myself from many people that I thought I loved," Colin said.

"Colin, do you remember what you told me?" Kiz asked.

"Yeah. I remember it like it was yesterday. You were standing at the crosswalk waiting to cross the street when my dad dropped me off at 6th & Hamilton. I waved to you to wait for me before you crossed the street. You did wait, as you did every school day since we were in first grade. I'm still amazed how quickly we bonded considering how different our backgrounds. My dad was determined to have his kids experience the public school system. He felt personally iso- lated himself coming from so much wealth that he missed something in life… he always felt too protected. He wanted something different for his kids. My mom and dad agreed to let the kids attend public elementary school, but high school would be private schools. So, my dad would drive me into the neighborhood to this great diverse elementary school where the foundation of my values was to develop. My parents kept a house on 2nd Street, an old family mansion, and another home in New York. I later learned the reason for my father's travel the night we stole the gun was because he was in New York where family businesses are is located. Anyway, my sister and brother both went to Hamilton, and later Camp Curtin before being shipped off to private schools after the incidents in Harrisburg. And, as you already know, I left Hamilton and went to Steinbeck in Boston, where I saw you again a couple years after the incident," Colin said.

"So, do you remember what you told me?" Kiz repeated.

"Yea. We were walking across 6th Street after the cross guard let us past. I whispered in your ear that I had a secret to tell you. You told me to meet you at the water fountain at recess. Colin continued, "When I met you later that morning, here's what I told you.

"'Kiz, I heard some men at my house talking about killing some people because they were afraid too much power or something was being given to the Negros in town. And I heard one of the men say my sister told his daughter that a few black boys from Cumberland Street tried to rape her at the river.' The men were arguing because of a kidnaping or something else over on Cumberland Street; they were not sure who was to do what. My dad wasn't home… he rented the lower level of the mansion to a social club, mostly men.

"Our family never used the front entrance… we used a rear entrance and occupied an entirely different portion of the Hugh mansion. Over the years, I had found secret ways to navigate the through the old place and would listen to conversations all the time through a crack in the wall between the stairwells that connected the properties although the access was locked and boarded-up I could still hear the conversations," Colin said.

"Did you ever tell your parents what you heard?" Kiz asked.

"Yes, I told my dad a few months ago what I heard. This was after a lot of therapy, I really didn't realize how the information I had would impact so many people," Colin said.

"So, Kiz, the reason I wanted to meet with you is to say how sorry I am that your family was so wrongfully impacted and caught-up in these racist and unthinkable acts. I'm so sorry," Colin said.

Kiz sat still and started to remember the conversation but not exactly how Colin had shared. So many years had passed, and they were seven-year-old kids. She remembered listening but not connecting the overheard conversation to her family that day. It would be years later after recalling that conversation that she began to make some connections to what a little girl had told her about an overheard conversation.

Kiz knew there was a lot more to her kidnapping and her mother's death. She didn't understand the role the corpses played in the events of that day. Kiz looked at Colin and just as she began to speak, things began to become clearer. For the first time in a long time, she remembered the corpses' warning. "Run Kizzy, run, run," the corpses said as they disintegrated in front of her.

"Colin, do you remember what the men looked like? If you had to describe them, could you?" Kiz asked, sounding desperate.

"Interesting you should ask that question, Kiz. Dad asked me the same question when I told him the story," Colin said.

"And the answer is?" Kiz asked, still sounding desperate.

"Dad had me meet with some men who took a statement then asked me to describe the men. I did my best to give them what I remembered. Again, it was a crack in the wall. I saw five men sitting at a table, lots of smoke from cigars, liquor was on the table and the room was well lit. I think they were playing cards. The windows were open. I remembered that because one of the men stood up and walked over to the window. He closed the windows because the sheers were blowing rapidly and distracting the men. The man shut the window directly in front of the men and pulled the sheers apart to a full view of the river. The other men put their cards down and walked over to the window to take a look at something the man was pointing at. When they turned around to sit back down at the long table, that's when I saw their faces. I later gave those descriptions to my dad's personal attorney when we met," Colin said.

"Wow… Colin you've kept this information for years, and like me, didn't know what to do with it. Or, how it was connected to other events that happened. We both know the truth about what happened at the River. We were there. Do you think your sister really lied about that?" Kiz said.

"No, she didn't lie. I asked her about that when I saw her a few years ago. She told me when she told Belinda, her friend, about the incident at the river. She told her about the white boy who tried to rape her and the black boys trying to help. Belinda's dad was running for City Attorney at the time and was running a campaign of hate. Remember this was during a very racially divided period in our history. Instead of stating the truth, Belinda's father turned the story around to rouse up the racial divide in the community. The good news was he lost the race. What harm he did in the process is unmeasured. He never used my sister's name but talked a lot about the incident at the river to a minor who he could not name," Colin said.

"Bastards. I'm gonna find these men, all of them, and prosecute them for murder – the killing of my mother. And I'm going to do everything I can to learn the identities of the corpses if it takes the rest of my life. Somehow, I think the two things are connected," Kiz said.

"Then you must believe your kidnapping is related too?" Colin said.

"Oh, hell yeah. And I will connect all the dots and bring to justice the men responsible for those events during that crazy week in 1952," Kiz said.

"How long have you been thinking about this Kiz?" Colin asked.

Kiz picked-up the knife next to her sandwich and flipped it on the end and started tapping on the table. She leaned forward, slightly rising from the chair to get closer to Colin who was sitting right across from her. Suddenly, her eyes narrowed, and she looked beyond Colin at something in the distance. Then she slowly sat back down.

"Are you okay, Kiz," a concerned Colin asked.

"Yes, yes, I thought I saw someone I knew over there standing next to the tree behind that bench," Kiz said, wondering if, after all these years the Watcher had returned.

Colin turned around to look. But she didn't see anyone or anything unusual. It was a busy place and lots of people milling around, some in a hurry and others lingering around. After all it was New York City.

"I'm sorry Colin, what did you ask me?" she said as she stirred the straw in her glass before taking another sip of her soda. Kiz was deep in thought and wondering how much to share with Colin. Seeing the Watcher standing there was a warning of some kind. He always came to protect her from evil.

"How long have you been thinking about the summer of 1952?" Colin repeated.

"Off and on ... mostly, I've let that day go," Kiz said. "You know, Colin, they never did find out who murdered my mom or a motive, and the corpses were never identified – no one ever claimed anyone missing. Don't you think that's strange?" Kiz said.

"Not really, given the times. But you did the right thing, Kiz. You moved on with your life and you've never looked back. You have a great story. Left Harrisburg, ended up in private schools and now about to enter Harvard Law School – that's fantastic," Colin said.

"Okay, enough of the really serious stuff ... how's your love life?" Kiz asked Colin.

"Oh no, not fair. You go first. I'm the one who asked for this get together," Colin said laughing.

The two old friends caught up on the new men in their lives and chatted some more about what was next for them. They promised to stay in touch. Colin promised to send Kiz the name of the person her father had her meet with. They exchanged contact information once again and gave each other a bear hug and kisses. They held unto each other tightly for precious seconds, and any stranger seeing the embrace and raw emotion between the two women could easily see the deep affection between them. When they let go, both Colin and Kiz looked deeply into each other's eyes. They both knew this was goodbye as they walked away in different directions without a word, never to see or speak to each other ever again.

Chapter 10

Landing Enterprise and Shadow Corporation

W inston Barksdale and Carlton Rankin started Landing Enterprise in the 1920s as an automated business transaction company. Winston Barksdale and Carlton Rankin were young men working out of Winston's family guest house in the Hamptons when they founded the company. Landing Enterprise would evolve to become a successful computer tabulating company with great interest in computing technology.

Both Winston and Carlton's fathers had been prominent slave owners from Louisiana and Georgia; the families' wealth had its origins in the agricultural economy of those state. The Lewis' family would later own Shadow Corporation, another successful computing company and fearless competitor and enemy.

In the late 1800s, the patriarchs of the Lewis and Barksdale and Rankin families were accused of brutally raping a slave girl named Genevieve who practiced witchcraft – the slave girl gave birth to a baby girl as a result of the rape – the child grew up with a mental disorder. Genevieve was said to have placed a curse on her daughter and the two men who had raped her. The rumor during the time and later in the small town where Genevieve would raise her daughter was that Genevieve (the witch) had cursed her daughter and any children born to the daughter would be cursed.

Years later, a granddaughter named Marylee Landrieu was born. The Lewis, Barksdale, and Rankin men friendships ended as a result of a series of strange deaths and suicides associated with the rape. These deaths became the legacy of these families – and the corpse of the dead was frequently offered as gifts for the sins of the fathers – a redemption ritual that continued in these families. The ultimate sacrifice would be Genevieve's granddaughter – Marylee Landrieu, the child who offered the grandmother eternal life.

The story of the curse was well known and documented in the families' history. And so, the competitiveness between Landing and Shadow started out of a need for redemption and dominance. Old friendships ended.

Landing Enterprise believed their future was in the acquisition of the best and brightest minds. The company tried at the very beginning to define predictive modeling and analytics as a competitive advantage for their future. Winston and Carlton believed whoever controlled the flow of information and built the infrastructure to hold information would rule the world. Shadow Corporation had the same vision.

Both organizations had been challenged to establish the right structures and mechanisms to support their vision. In fact, the solution was not yet developed so the understanding of how to get there was fair game for anyone to take the lead. Landing and Shadow were sourcing the world looking for the best talent they could find to help build what they felt was the future of their industry.

Landing Enterprise, 1955

Winston Barksdale didn't care much for the three new independent board members who were replacing his old conspirators on the Landing Board; the friends had been together for over forty years in various business relationships; now they like him would be leaving the board due to health concerns and age limitations. All three of the new members – Paul Smith, Michael Kelly, and Forge Malone – had served on the board of Landing Enterprise for over twenty years; the remaining four seasoned board members – Dawson Kelly, Greg Knowles, Race Barron, and Frank Connor – were also longtime friends and business associates of Winston and Carlton. There was a clear shift happening on the board and within the company. Succession planning, technology and inclusions were dominating the conversations. The three new independent directors were coming in from outside of the industry and represented new and unfamiliar voices – Carmen Williams, an African American woman recently retired from a premier New York advertising firm, Ellis De Castro, former CEO of a large technology investment consultancy, and Paul Carlisle, a prominent university professor and author of several books focused on high finance and commercial viability in biotech and research.

Winston felt the direction these new directors would lead the company was not what he and Carlton Rankin had imagined over thirty years ago. Even more concerning was the proprietary nature of Landing and the secrets it held close to just a small circle of confidants. Winston did not know these new directors and felt he could not trust them. All three were way too liberal for his taste. Winston's daughter Margie Francis Barksdale would own a significant portion of Landing's stock upon his death along with his grandson Clay Barksdale. The Rankin legacy was similarly spit between surviving siblings, and Colin's parents were distant heirs to the fortune unknown to the family. The two patriarchs Winston Barksdale and Carlton Rankin were still controlling things at Landing although things were changing and a younger generation was making key decisions, and because of new technologies it was a very different organization than when the two men imagined the company.

"Who the hell are they, Carlton? We don't know these people and we have too much at stake to bring people this close to our business without knowing some secret we can hold against them," Winston ranted while pacing the floor and smoking a cigar. "I just can't believe you want this. I just can't. Our fathers would.... What are you looking at Carlton?" Winston said as he noticed Carlton with something flashing in his hand.

"The future! Yeah, the three new members are bringing different voices to our board – but we need them here for other reasons. You see this gadget in my hand, Winston? Well, it's the future. How quickly we – Landing – can figure out how to get this integrated with other information and processes we're working on remains the key to our control of the world's commerce," Carlton said.

"What is it exactly?" Winston asked as he placed his cigar on the ashtray and picked-up his glasses to take a closer look.

"It's a chip. Inside it contains trillions of bits of information. But what's missing is the ability to integrate and connect the pieces. Right now, it's just information, a big step but there's much more to come," Carlton continued.

"And the Caldwell girl?" Winston whispered, "is the key to our future?"

"Yes, she's more important than ever. But the methods we've used over the years are not working. We're still unable to reproduce the unique genetic traits she holds," Carlton continued.

The two men walked over to the window and looked out at the new construction surrounding them.

"You see those three buildings," Carlton asked as he pointed at the scaffolds adjacent to the three new buildings being built around Landing's headquarters. "All three of those buildings will be the home to biotechnology and computer software companies. We can't let that happen," Carlton said as he turned to face his partner.

Winston nodded, and without words he turned to looking at the buildings and thought, 'we are running out of time! Perhaps Carlton was right – the benefit of having three new members on the board during this next stage of growth was critical.' He just felt like he was losing control. He had spent his entire career with Landing Enterprise. He believed every word his father had told him about the genetic traits that would change the world.

The war or competition between his father and Mark Lewis, the founder of Shadow Corporation was all he had known. The two men (thus families) hated each other. And the reasons why had a lot to do with the old men's childhood in Louisiana. Both of their fathers were prominent slave owners and both men were involved with a particular slave woman who was owned by the Landrieu Lewis plantation, later Shadow Corporation. The slave woman was into witch-craft and voodoo. She had a child, and the child was said to be of Landrieu blood, but Landrieu denied the child. The slave woman was said to have placed a curse on the Landrieu Lewis and Barksdale men, blaming them for her unwanted pregnancy.

The company was now at an important stage in its growth – needing more aggressive international and critical talent to help capture and dominate key markets for analytics and pre-dictive modeling. The company was already a major partner with the US military as was their major competitor, Shadow Corporation. But the two organizations operating models were very different, and the reputations were different. Both

Shadow and Landing had lost key recruits over the years, but both grew in spite of the lost.

Dr. Kline, who delivered Kiz Lamise Caldwell, was a medical student at Harvard in the 1930s, and he became interested in the link between genetics and intelligence. Dr. Kline developed a series of unscientific noninvasive tests for infants that he used in medical school to test his theory. He tracked these kids for the first four years of their lives to determine if his hypothesis was correct. In almost all the cases, he was proven wrong. Then in 1945, there was a little girl name Kiz Lamise Caldwell he delivered who showed signs his theory was correct. Although an unusual situation with the nurse at her birth sent red flags that there was something special about the little girl when she was almost kidnapped from the hospital. Dr. Kline knew he had to protect the child; which he did and would continue to do for as long as he could.

Dr. Kline was approached by a friend from medical school who wanted to tell him about two offers he had to work in the private sector as a research scientist for a company called the Shadow Corporation. Dr. Kline remembered getting calls from another company and the federal government for interesting opportunities. He never thought about any of them. He knew he wanted to be a practicing physician, although he did enjoy the research aspect of his training.

So, that's when he decided to follow up on two inquiries he was receiving from two companies, Landing Enterprise and Shadow Corporation. Dr. Kline decided he would pursue both opportunities because of his keen interest in research. He would later choose to work for Landing Enterprise and continue his practice as a physician at Harrisburg Hospital.

Chapter 11

Shadow Corporation

1955

"Would you like a cup of coffee, Mrs. Dinkins?" the receptionist asked.

"Yes, thank you," Marylee replied.

Jane, the receptionist, was straight out of Shadow's playbook. Formal, tight lipped, dark blue suit with a high-collared white blouse and a string of pearls, low-heel navy pumps and stockings.

Marylee sat up straight as she looked around the room, remembering the first time she was there. She must have been nineteen or twenty years old. She had just left Louisiana and was looking for a job. Her grandmother's sister gave her a number to call in New York and that number landed her at Shadow Corporation; where she was introduced to an old man who sat down with her and read the letter inside the envelop from Marylee's great aunt who insisted she only share the letter with Mr. Lewis. The content was about redemption.

Marylee recalled Mr. Lewis staring at her after he read the letter, carefully studying her face as if he saw something familiar and appeared frightened. Marylee often wondered how the old man knew so much about her family. She got a job at Shadow Corporation on that same day she met with the old man, Mr. Lewis, and received her first assignment. A man name Richard Dinkins who owned the brothel on 7th Ave – she was to get him to fall in love with her. She would be on the payroll of Shadow Corporation and her broader assignment and road toward redemption would become clear; meanwhile Shadow enrolled her in college to get more education. Marylee happily accepted, believing she understood the path this assignment would put her on.

Many years had passed. She needed to get back in the game; her life had been upended by the events in Harrisburg and Kizzy Caldwell's kidnapping three years ago. She knew it wouldn't be easy to get a new assignment, but she was ready to forget and move on. Redemption was still her goal, and she could not get that without the connection to Kizzy Caldwell.

"Would you like some more coffee, Mrs. Dinkins?" the receptionist asked.

"No, thank you," Marylee responded as a buzzer rang at the receptionist's desk.

"Yes, Mr. Lewis, I'll let her know," the receptionist said.

Jane stood and walked over to Marylee. She was embarrassed to deliver the message that Mr. Lewis was not available to see her.

"I'm sorry, Mrs. Dinkins. Mr. Lewis is running late and is unable to meet with you and there is no one else available. He asked that I express his sincere apologies for the inconvenience."

Marylee was surprised. She stood, thinking to herself. *So, this is the price for losing Kizzy.* Would the old man and the organization ever forgive her? She had lost everything.

"Mrs. Dinkins, may I show you the way out?" Jane continued as she stood near the door.

"No, thank you, I think I can find my way," Marylee said.

Marylee heard the door to the inner office open as she walked out. She continued walking toward the elevator of the old stately building on Broadway and 5th Avenue. She was thinking how weird the encounter was and why she was summoned back there in the first place.

What would be Shadow's next move? She felt weak and lost. As she walked out of the building, her thoughts quickly moved to how much she loved New York and how much longer she would stay at the hotel. It had been three years since she moved there. Now she needed something more stable. She needed to find an apartment and a job.

Marylee closed her eyes and stood at the entry of Shadow Corporation for just a moment, hoping to be called back inside for the meeting with Mr. Lewis.

"Marylee? Is that you? Hey, it's me, Paul France! Do you remember me from Chloe's and City College? Girl, you look, well, ridiculously proper in that outfit. How are you doing?"

Marylee was almost speechless. "Paul?"

"Girl, the last thing any of us heard, was you had gone off and got married. Where have you been all these years?" Paul asked.

"Paul Nance, I'll be damned. I'm doing fine, in New York on a little business. How are you doing?" Marylee asked as she moved away from the entry to Shadow Corporation.

The two old friends embraced and laughed as they talked over each other with genuine excitement.

"Well, you can see I'm fine as ever, but girl you don't look too good. Now, we go way back. How are you doing? Remember this is Paul you are talking to!"

Marylee smiled. "Paul, I really need to go. Sorry to be in a hurry but…."

"Oh, hell no. You can't just push me off like that Marylee. Come on, join me for lunch, or a drink or something – dinner maybe? Where are you going in such a hurry?" Paul pleaded.

Marylee paused. "Okay Paul, I'd like that, and I do have some time before I need to get to an appointment later this evening. Where do you want to go?" Marylee asked.

"Well, I've been working down here on Wall Street for a few years now. You won't believe this. I'm a broker for a top financial house on Wall Street, a long way from the days at Chloe's. Anyway, I know the perfect spot. How much time do you have?" Paul asked.

Marylee looked at Paul. "I am flexible, I can get to my other appointment tomorrow. Nothing was confirmed," Marylee said in an embarrassed tone.

"Let's head over to P.J. Clarke's. Drinks are on me," Paul said as he held up his right hand in her face. "Not another word, Marylee."

Paul hailed a taxicab for the two of them. They laughed and chatted about old times as they took the short trip to the popular bar. Marylee found it strange that Paul didn't ask her why she was in New York and on Wall Street.

They had been the best of friends, until Marylee's grandmother died. Something changed, and then she became serious with Richard Dinkins and everything they had as friends disappeared. Paul always wondered what happened to change her life so drastically.

The restaurant was not crowded yet, but in a few hours, it would be filled with the cocktail crowd. A too familiar dark bar with mahogany wood paneled walls, oak floors, a circular bar with black high-top chairs with red leather seats. The marble counter and tabletops gave an upscale feel with the mirrored ceiling giving an illusion of a much larger space. There were six private booths surrounding the bar area, with black leather seats and mahogany tables against a stained-glass wall. The lights were low, and the room echoed with the sound of contemporary jazz. An old juke box and pictures of celebrities and politicians adorned the paneled walls.

Marylee was suddenly feeling tired, and ready to explode. She needed to dump years of frustration, and Paul was there all ears. They both ordered a whiskey sour each to get started.

Marylee studied Paul carefully, thinking as she sipped the cocktail. She thought, after all these years how did he just happen to run into her by accident outside of Shadow's headquarters on Wall Street. Was it really just a coincidence or something else? She had to be careful and learn more about him; it had been a long time since she had seen him last.

"A toast to old friends and the future!" Marylee offered as she lifted her glass.

"Yes, I'll toast to that and our renewed friendship," Paul responded as both glasses touched.

Paul lingered a bit too long staring into the bottom of his glass… thinking about two old friends about to go on a journey of betrayal and danger; somehow their history together might have predicted this moment.

"So, tell me Marylee, what's happened since we last saw each other?" Paul asked.

"Oh Paul, I don't even know where to begin. How long has it been, thirteen, fifteen years?" Marylee said.

"Close. We heard you got married to the man who owned the Club and left New York. I think that's the last time anyone heard anything about you. You and I lost touch right after your grandma passed away. The last time we spoke, you were headed back to Louisiana to her funeral. You never called or returned my calls after that," Paul said.

Marylee decided to test him. There was something making her uncomfortable. Why did he bring up her grandmother? Out of nowhere, Marylee said, "I left him in Pennsylvania and now I need a place to stay. Can you help me?" She thought there was a slight smirk on his face when she asked the question.

"Of course, I can help you. How soon do you need a place to stay?" Paul asked, as he thought, 'how lucky am I … she trusts me.'

"How about tomorrow?" Marylee asked.

"No problem. Give me a few minutes to make a quick phone call," Paul said as he stood up and headed for the phone booth in the back of the restaurant.

"Wait. How much will it cost me? Right now, I don't have a job. I'll need to start looking for a job soon too," Marylee said.

Paul looked at his old friend. "Let me help you, Marylee. What kind of work are you looking for?" he asked as he sat back down.

Marylee stared at him for a while before speaking. "I don't really know, maybe finance or accounting work?"

Marylee didn't know what to expect based on the visit to the Shadow's headquarters earlier, and now Paul! She was feeling something wasn't right. But why? And how was Paul Nance involved?

"Okay," Paul said as he got back up. "I'm going to make a few calls right now, Marylee. Go ahead and order some food. Nothing is off limits. You must be starving. I'm starving."

Marylee yelled out as Paul walked quickly toward the back of the restaurant toward the telephone booth, "How about another drink straight up?"

He never heard her call out, as the popular bar was beginning to fill up with the pre-dinner crowd.

Marylee sat in the booth holding the glass of whiskey as she thought about Shadow and the secret account that Shadow gave all its connectors as they worked on cases; connectors were considered employees and their life was always in service to Shadow, especially hers. She had only used the account to make small payments to two companies where she bought stock. Otherwise, the account showed minimum withdrawals and large deposits annually over 15 years.

The account balance was over a million dollars. Marylee was always a shrewd businesswoman – even when she and Richard ran the brothel on the eastside. It was Marylee who handled the books and managed the money. They sold the business to local thugs for $200,000 in cash and moved to Harrisburg right after handing over the deed. Marylee was thinking about the joint account with Richard and how she had walked away from that money and the life with him.

Marylee was actually a wealthy woman and could have used the savings from her Shadow account to live comfortably in New York without a job for a while longer if she decided to do so. But Marylee had other plans. She expected her last check from Shadow to be deposited in a few weeks. The contract called for a three-year grace period after an assignment was terminated before payments stopped. Shadow used this incentive to retain its employees. Generally, the last check included what they considered unusual expenses and separation pay. If a connector was lucky enough to get a reassignment, the negotiations for pay started all over again with the new assignment.

Marylee never told Richard about the secret bank account she opened before they married and stayed at the Bank of New York. The account was set up in her maiden name Marylee Charles Landrieu and had been there for over 15 years. She changed her name in her early twenties to that of her slave master grandfather from Louisiana. She thought of her grandmother and the curse she had bestowed upon her unwilling mother and the unborn child she carried. Marylee's drive for redemption would not end now. She was on a mission to change the preannounced destiny that shadowed her entire life to this point. Shadow Corporation was a critical component to redemption. She would use her maiden name, Landrieu going forward.

"Hello, hello, hey," Paul said as he reached over to touch Marylee's hand. "Wow, you were deep in thought about something."

"Paul, I'm sorry, just got a lot on my mind. When did you get back? Do I have an apartment or any good news?" Marylee asked.

"Well, I do have some good news and bad news," Paul began. "Should I start with the good news first?"

"Why not? Go ahead," Marylee said as she looked at him and yet beyond him, her hands nervously tapping the side of her glass, an old habit that had returned in the recent month.

Paul picked up his glass and took a sip of the Jack Daniels. He knew he would need more than a sip – something he had controlled for the most part. But he had a feeling this evening would be different, and he would need more than a sip.

"Well, I got you an apartment on the upper west side if you want it," Paul said. "The apartment can be ready in a few days. And it's fully furnished. You can lease it for up to three years for $500 a month. The owner of the duplex is moving upstate and retiring from his company. A friend of mine at the firm is married to his nephews' daughter. That's how I made the connection."

"Incredible. Paul, I can't believe this! This is remarkable. How could this even be possible? Are you sure?" Marylee asked. She knew Paul was lying. She had a very good sense about people and knew this entire episode was a bit too convenient.

"Yes, it's incredible, in fact, I was trying to figure out how to give you my place and take on the apartment on the upper west side. If you want to trade, let me know," Paul said.

Both of them laughed at the suggestion.

"No, I'm interested," Marylee said. "What's the bad news? Don't tell I'll need to return to the old days and set-up a sophisticated whore house on the upper west side?" Marylee said while she continued to laugh, watching Paul's reaction at the same time.

"No, not that. Okay, here's the bad news," Paul said with a slight hesitation. You have to accept the offer tonight, site unseen. And move into the apartment (actually duplex) on a specific date and timeframe. I'll give you the information later. The building is in a highly secured area and surrounded by international business executives and security professionals," Paul said as he looked intensely at Marylee.

"So, are you saying my moving in and out of the building will be monitored?" Marylee asked.

"Yes. And, I'm saying to you confidently as a longtime friend that you will have an opportunity to also work for some very important people who are working on secret projects from around the world. Marylee, I don't know much more than that," Paul said as he reached for the menu and waved for the waitress.

"So, was that the bad news?" Marylee asked.

"No, there's more," Paul said.

Marylee braced herself for what she believed would be next. What came next, she could have imagined.

"Well, Paul what is it?" Marylee asked as the waitress walked over to the table.

"Good afternoon, folks. Can I get you another drink? We will be switching over to our evening and dinner menu in 15 minutes. You are welcome to stay here or move into the dining room if you plan to stay for dinner." The waitress looked at them both with a big smile.

Paul spoke up before Marylee had a chance to respond. "Yes, we are staying for dinner. We already have reservations."

"Great, sir, I'm happy to check on your reservation and make sure your table will be available," the waitress said as she took out a pad to write on.

"Yes, please do. The reservation is listed under Paul Nance for 5:45 p.m., a booth for three people in the private dining area," Paul said.

"Of course, Paul Nance, Shadow Corporation. I actually took the call myself earlier today from Emily over at Mr. Lewis's office. My name is Diane. Greta, our hostess, will be right back to re-confirm your reservation and when you are ready, she'll show you to the dining room."

Marylee could feel the tension inside of her jaw collapsing in her mouth against her grinding teeth as she tried hard not to react with emotion. Her hands rested tightly on each kneecap, both feet were digging into the hard wood floor, she avoided direct eye contact with Paul, and then she finally spoke.

"Is that the bad news Paul? You work for Shadow Corporation? What do you want Paul? Why am I here?" Marylee asked in the calm, direct, and intense manner she was known for.

"Sir, my name is Greta. I'm the hostess this evening. I just want to welcome you to P.J. Clarke's and let you know that everything will be ready for your evening with us. Meanwhile, please relax and enjoy a complementary drink on the house. We'll seat you in the main dining room at 5:45pm," Greta said as she moved away from the booth.

Paul welcomed the interruptions, as it gave him time to think about what he would say to Marylee. "Thank you," he said as the hostess left the booth.

Paul continued, "Yes, I work for the Shadow Corporation. Shortly after you left New York, I left the bank. Over the years I was promoted several times. In recent years I served as VP of Financial Services for Shadow Corporation. About ten years ago, I was routinely reviewing accounts payable in preparation for an audit. I noticed there were employee accounts and deposits that were being made under a unique accounting code. The accounts were being charged to a department titled special employees.

"So, I had my assistant do some digging and let me know what she found out. Well, what I learned wasn't too unusual, but I just happened to eyeball the report. That's when I saw a name that caught my attention – Marylee Charles Landrieu. The name of my first customer at Bank of New York."

Paul continued. "I thought, this can't be a coincidence. Why would Marylee's name show up on Shadow's special accounts ledger consistently over years. And of course, the only thing I could think of was Chloe's, the brothel, and maybe Marylee had continued to provide some service to the corporation, outside of New York." Paul stopped and took another sip of his whiskey.

As Marylee listened to Paul, she wondered how much he knew. Or was he waiting for her to fill in the blanks? She sat there taking intermittent sips of her whiskey. She couldn't help thinking this was going to be an interesting and long evening. She thought, why a booth for three?

Marylee looked at Paul and asked, "So, Paul, bumping into me earlier today – that was no accident, right?"

"No, Marylee. Mr. Lewis called me to say an old friend of mine just left his office… he asked me to surprise you. Then he told you you might need a place to stay and a job. If so, he told me who to call. He then said, he would explain everything tonight at dinner," Paul said.

Marylee was stunned. She had so many questions. "How did Mr. Lewis know you knew me?"

Paul began, "Marylee, I honestly do not know. What I do know is there are no secrets at Shadow Corporation. Maybe they knew I was tracking your account and the years of the expenses, and perhaps I asked just a few too many questions about your account. So, my guess is somebody at the company did a check on my background and discovered the connection."

Paul and Marylee saw Greta approaching and stopped talking. Both looked up at the jovial and attractive hostess, waiting for further instructions.

"Excuse me, your table is available, and the rest of your party has arrived," Greta said.

The dining room was large – warmly light, typical New York. The tables were adorned with white tablecloths and perfect table settings. The floors were all highly polished oak, and the walls were mahogany paneled with pictures of famous guests who had eaten in the restaurant over the years. A highly polished black Steinway piano sat off to the side of the room on a riser, making viewing and listening from any place in the room possible. The jazz pianist played softly in the background. The wooden window shutters were tilted open to give a sense of the outdoors meeting the intimacy of the dining room. The room was beginning to fill with folks coming in for the early dinner reservation.

Marylee and Paul were guided to their table – were Mr. Lewis sat while two other men stood at a table near theirs. The hostess gestured toward a chair for Marylee, while it was apparent the table was set for two.

"Good evening, Mr. Lewis," Paul said as he and Marylee approached the table

"Hello Paul, Ms. Dinkins or Landrieu, please have a seat," Mark Lewis said as he nodded toward the chair at the table where he sat. "Paul, please join the others," Mark Lewis ordered as he turned his attention to Marylee. The hostess took Paul over to a table on the other side of the room where the other two men were seated. Paul later learned the two men were Mr. Lewis's security personnel.

Marylee looked at Mark Lewis. It had been years since she had seen him. The years were not kind to him. He had aged much beyond his years and the once tall, handsome, blond, young man who sat next to his father during her visit to Shadow was now an overweight, greying, and worn looking man with the look of someone with untold secrets and a lack of joy for life.

"Hello Mark," Marylee said as she continued to explore the stranger across from her, the person she once knew so well before his deep involvement in his family's business Shadow Corporation. She would meet him at the brothel. He was a regular then – handsome, a loner, kind, and her special friend. She often wondered what would become of him. She later learned of his wealth and family connections. They would spend hours talking about life and the paths they both had taken; her grandmother and his grandfather's connection, the redemption path she was on. It was Mark who got her the job at Shadow and helped make the connection between the little girl in Harrisburg – Kiz Caldwell – and Marylee's freedom.

Mark was born into Shadow and knew one day he would be in charge. His first test or assignment was to befriend Marylee and make the connection between her and the girl. After Marylee was given the order, she never saw Mark again, nor did she know Mark was the Mr. Lewis she was dealing with for the past twenty years.

Mark sat there quietly for a moment. His rugged handsome faced showed the signs of a lonely man – perhaps someone with a lot of regrets and pain.

"Hello, Marylee. You look well. I apologize for not meeting with you earlier. But a less intimidating setting would be better given our history and the nature of this meeting," Mark Lewis said.

"Are you okay? Can I order you another drink?" Mark continued, as he motioned the server to the table. "Shall I order us a bottle of wine before dinner?"

"Yes, that would be fine. Red please," Marylee said.

Chapter 12

Kizzy and Clay

1967

Kiz Lamise Caldwell was twenty-two years old, had just been accepted into law school for the coming year, and was in the process of deciding her summer internship. The choices were narrowed down to two prestigious Boston law firms: Larkins, Cantor & Brown and Streets & Drum, or two well-known and growing New York companies: Landing Enterprise and Shadow Corporation. All four of these organizations were aggressively recruiting her and other first-year law students from the top law schools. She had accepted a full scholarship to Harvard Law School, and Boston was familiar to her since she spent the last ten years there in private school and had attended undergraduate at Harvard.

Carmen, Kiz's sister, had encouraged her to consider someplace different like Yale or Columbia, or come back home to Penn. Kiz decided to stick with Harvard.

The internship during the summer was important because it could possibly be the place she would end up after law school; so, the connections and opportunity to work with some of the most exciting lawyers in the country made the choice of where to work even more complicated.

Kiz had wanted all her life to be a lawyer, law professor and judge in that order. Even as a little girl she would lead arguments, defend her position based on facts not emotions, and teach others through presentation of the evidence; often, she was selected as the one to make the final argument. The kids at her boarding school would call it Judge Kizzy's Court.

She decided to focus on corporate and anti-trust law.

Two months later

Clay Barksdale, Jr., a young corporate attorney working for his uncle's company, Landing Enterprise, was thirty-three. He was deciding on a political career and planning to run for public office in a few years. He was deeply concerned with civil rights and social justice in the country and wanted to help change the system; he thought public office was the best route for him to make a difference. Working in his family business was okay, too, although it wasn't exactly where his heart was. His grandfather and mother would be proud of him for following the family tradition.

In 1967, Clay was attending a conference in Boston when he decided to visit some old law school friends from Yale who were working at Larkins, Cantor & Brown, a top litigation firm in the country. He was consulting with them on a case being filed in New York.

Clay arrived a little early for his appointment, so he decided to use the firm's law library while he waited.

As he walked toward the library, two young women were in front of him. He could tell from the conversation that they were both college kids, maybe interns. They were debating the pros and cons of Yale versus Harvard. Clay was amazed by the maturity of the conversation and the brilliance of their arguments.

The three of them arrived at the library at the same time. Clay reached out to open the door for the young women. He then asked, almost amused, "So, who's going to Yale and who's going to Harvard?"

Kiz turned slightly as she responded, "I'm Harvard and she's Yale."

The three went into the library, and the interns went their separate ways while Clay went to the law librarian to check on some materials.

"Good afternoon, I am attorney Clay Barksdale from Landing Enterprise in New York. I think you are holding some documents for me."

The law librarian turned to check the holding materials. "Yes, Mr. Barksdale we have your materials here. Please check them and sign here if everything is okay," the librarian said.

Clay took a quick look, nodded and signed. He still had some time before his meeting, so he sat down and began to review the materials. The library was busy with clerks, interns, lawyers and special assistants going in and out. A part of the library was always noisy just as at the library at Landing; and technology was changing the industries. He wondered how long before these big firm libraries would go away.

"Hey, Clay Barksdale what are you doing here?" A familiar voice greeted him. "You finally came to your senses and agreed to accept our offer." The man smiled broadly as he affectionately slapped Clay's right arm. "And how are your uncle and the rest of the folks down there in New York doing?"

Kizzy was stacking books right behind the men and overheard the exchange. It was clear to her that the tall handsome younger man could not remember Mr. Larkins' name. So, Kizzy decided to intervene.

"My uncle he's doing great. Thank you, sir, for asking about him. I'll let him know you asked about him," Clay said.

"Excuse me Mr. Larkins, I'm sorry to interrupt you." Kizzy handed the firm's lead partner and founder a book. "I hope this is the edition you've been searching for, Mr. Larkins," Kizzy said with a smile.

Mr. Larkins turned his attention to the book that Kizzy handed him. He smiled broadly. "And," he asked, "where did you find it?"

Kizzy smiled and just said, "I accidently took it home to read. I didn't realize it was so special. I should have asked first."

"Are you the brilliant intern that everyone's talking about, the young lady headed to my alma mater, Harvard, in a few weeks?" Larkins said.

"Thank you, Mr. Larkins." Kiz turned to leave without acknowledging much more.

"Wait. I want to introduce you to the son of my dearest friend and oldest rival." Mr. Larkins turned to Clay. "Clay Barksdale, Jr., I want you to meet Larkins, Cantor & Brown's star intern." Mr. Larkins had clearly forgotten Kiz's name.

"Kiz Lamise Caldwell," Kiz said as she quickly extended her hand and for the first time looked at him directly in the face.

"What the hell's the matter with you son? You never saw a beautiful young woman before?" Larkins spouted as he introduced Kiz and Clay.

Before Clay could respond, a young woman interrupted them with a book cart. Or, as Clay would later say, she rescued him from a major embarrassment.

The first time they met, Kiz was seven years old, and Clay was eighteen.

Clay remembered Kiz's name; he never forgot the little girl that he met at his grandfather's farmhouse in Pennsylvania with his old friend Mason.

Kiz had a feeling of familiarity. There was something about this stranger that for the first time caused her to think about her protector, the Watcher.

Chapter 13

Forgiveness, Love, and Purpose

Forgiveness, 1977

Forgiveness was almost too much to ask of a young girl, but as the years moved on and memories began to fade, the young girl became a woman and life moved forward. She tried to forgive but knew she had not done so entirely. For her it would be a continuing journey. The biggest hurt was not so much the death of her mother or the kidnapping during her childhood, crimes that would never be solved, but the betrayal by loved ones.

Betrayal by those you love was the most painful and difficult to forget and forgive. The Colin Rankin, Marylee Dinkins, and Clay Barksdale betrayals were the worst.

Kiz wanted to believe so badly that Colin was truly sorry, but her loyalties were beyond their friendship and Colin was a survivor. But to lose a friend without saying goodbye, to lose them knowing the regrets and misunderstandings built an impenetrable wall between the two women. The face-to-face meeting between the two at the Tavern on the Green in New York that beautiful fall day didn't go well. The secrets were so deep that both of their hearts were still wounded by the tragedy of their youth, resulting in the absence of trust and respect. Time had separated them, but the space between them was now filled with the blurriness of time; though memories remained with moments overflowing with hope, those memories were only illusions soon to disappear.

Colin and Kiz had both walked away from that encounter wondering who the other was. They never spoke to each other again.

Kiz knew she had to find a way to forgive Colin that would help set her free. She looked at the card handed to her by Carla Rankin, Colin's sister, that day on a plane from Paris, a chance meeting that took place over four years ago. Still, she would look up the young woman while in Paris. Hopefully, the young woman would be open to meeting with her.

Paris 1996

The plane landed on time at Charles De Gaulle airport where Kiz had traveled to three or four times since she and Clay got married in 1968. She and Clay both decided Paris would be the perfect place for the romantic wedding, almost twelve years ago. Kiz learned so much about Clay and his family over the years, but sometimes she wondered if she ever really knew who he was. She knew this trip to Paris would be different. She understood so much more.

The drive to the hotel was uneventful, and she checked into the hotel, unpacked, and took a quick shower before meeting the other speakers for dinner. She would make the call to Carla Rankin using the number on the card given to her that day on the plane. Kiz had done some investigating into Carla's background after meeting her on the flight that day. And, over the past four years tracked her life. She was raised in France and lived with her father and his wife until recently. Carla was a lawyer practicing international law, was not married nor did she have any children.

After checking into her room Kiz decided to call Carla first.

The phone rang several times before the recorder went on. "Hello, this is Carla Rankin; at Rankin and Smith, Attorney at Law, I'm unable to take your call at the moment. But if you leave a message…." Suddenly, the recording was interrupted with, "Hello, Carla Rankin speaking, may I help you."

Carla's voice was rushed, and clearly, she was running to pick up the phone. A young lawyer chasing calls, not missing any opportunities for the potential of new business.

"Hello Carla," Kiz slightly paused before continuing. "Carla, I don't know if you will remember me. I sat next to you on a flight from New York to Paris about four years ago. You were coming from your sister's funeral in Los Angeles."

"Oh yes, I do remember you. You were the very kind woman who listened to me tell tales about my sister the entire flight. Oh, I can't forget that. You were so kind. Yes, I do remember that flight and meeting you, but please forgive me. I don't remember your name. Or, if I ever asked you your name," Carla said.

Kiz didn't know what to say. She had practiced over and over how she would tell Carla who she was, yet the words would not come out.

"Are you there... hello?"

"Yes, yes, I am still here. In fact, I'm in Paris this week for a conference and decided to stay a few extra days. I would love to meet up with you for coffee, lunch or dinner later this week if you are available. I'm staying at the Maison Alba Hotel Paris Celine," Kiz said.

Carla was intrigued by this stranger's boldness and wondered who she was. "Which conference are you attending?" Carla asked. "I'm attending a conference myself over the next couple days, so later this week would work out best for me. I'll have to call you back after I look at my schedule, but I'm sure I can find time for coffee."

"Great. I'm attending and speaking at the International Criminal Justice Forum. I'll look forward to hearing from you. Here's my number, and you can of course leave a message for me at the hotel. Nice to chat with you Carla. Oh, my name is Kiz Lamise Barksdale. Talk with you soon," Kizzy said as she hung the phone up and took a deep breath.

A few minutes later her phone rang. Kiz picked-up the phone up to hear a familiar voice on the other end.

"Hey, sweetheart, how did it go? Did you call her?" Clay asked.

"Oh Clay, I don't know. I just called her, and she'll call me back," Kiz said.

"Did she recognize your name?" Clay asked.

"I didn't wait to find out," Kiz said. "I told her my name at the end then hung up. We'll see if she calls back. Hey, let me check in and let's talk later."

"Sure, I'll call you tomorrow. Nothing urgent," Clay said.

Kiz was struck by his tone and the "nothing urgent," which meant something was on his mind.

"Clay, do you need to talk about anything?" Kiz asked

"Not now, sweetheart. I'll call you later. Get settled in and I'll call you tomorrow evening," Clay said.

"Are you sure?" Kiz asked.

"I'm sure, goodbye honey."

Kiz stood next to the desk in her hotel room thinking Clay's call was a bit weird. She thought about calling him back but realized it was late in the States, so she decided to settle into her first night in Paris.

Clay back in the States

Clay had reviewed the files sent to him by the legal department at Landing. He decided to make a visit to his Aunt Marge and share the recent information he had found. Aunt Marge was always a good listener and a terrific person to bounce ideas off; she asked challenging questions and was a thoughtful problem solver. In many ways Aunt Marge and Clay were best friends. Even as a college student he went to Marge Barksdale to talk when he decided not to marry Allison Rankin, and she told him point blank it would be a mistake. Others tried to encourage him to marry Allison because of business interests between the families.

Aunt Marge told Clay to follow his passion – have some fun and the right person will come along. Clay listened to his aunt Marge.

Clay's father would say over and over again, "how can you listen to a woman who never married, hates men, treat people with disrespect, and embarrasses the family whenever she can? I love my sister, but she's trouble Clay!"

"Leave the boy alone. He'll be okay," Clay's mother would counter with a slight wink in Clay's direction.

Clay knew his mother agreed with Aunt Marge. His mother would ask Clay all the time, "When did you last see your Aunt Marge? How is she doing?"

Clay smiled just thinking about his family. He loved them all. But they remained cool toward Kiz.

Clay tucked the file under his arm and headed toward the door. He really needed Marge to see the contents. He also decided to remove the duplicated file from his desk and lock the copy in his private safe before leaving the apartment.

Chapter 14

Highs and Lows

C arla listened to the plan Kiz had laid out and was intrigued. Kiz shared with her a meeting she was planning with investors while in Paris to attend the conference and wanted Carla to consider being a part of the investment. The idea of being a principal part of this unique team of investors was both energizing and appealing to Carla. She always wanted to belong to something important that would change the course of history.

"Ms. Kiz, I accept your offer to work with you on the legal, compliance and regulatory aspects of this venture. And, yes, I will attend the private dinner you have arranged with the potential investors and principals," Carla said.

"I'm delighted with your response, Carla. And to get started, I have this NDA for you to sign, once you read through the terms. Then we'll get started. By the way, you never asked how much you'll be compensated for this work," Kiz said.

"Well, I was going to get to that part, but you beat me to it," Carla stated.

"Your first lesson in business, Carla. Always know your worth. Don't let others define your value. They will always underestimate your worth," Kiz said as she looked directly at Carla.

Kiz continued, "Before you said yes, you should have asked the question, what does this mean financially to you and what's the long-term perspective for you owning a stake in the venture."

Carla so admired this woman. Not only because of what she read or what her sister had shared- but how authentic and inspiring she was. Carla felt like she had known Kiz her entire life.

"Okay. So where should I start?" Carla asked, somewhat perplexed and inspired by Kiz's bluntness regarding the lack of business acumen she had.

Kiz reached into the briefcase, pulled out an envelope and handed it to Carla.

"What is this?" Carla asked.

"Your NDA and my retainer offer to you for your service," Kiz said.

"Oh, yes of course," Carla said.

Kiz smiled, and then said, "If we are going to do this, I want to sit down with you and work out some details of the meeting with you and a few other items. I will also be bringing a few other people to a private meeting with you and me before we meet with the investors. So, the sooner you and I can agree on the terms of our business relationship the better."

Carla took the envelope and placed it next to her purse on the chair next to hers. She looked at the woman across from her and wondered, what was the real motive behind this level of generosity? The relationship with my sister ended long ago. There had to be another reason. She had to find out.

"Well, what do you think about wrapping things up for the night?" Kiz asked.

Nodding in agreement, Carla stood up and the two women left the restaurant, said their goodbyes and agreed to talk again the following week to finalize a go or no-go strategy.

Kiz felt positive about the exchange with Carla. There was so much more to learn about the young woman. But Kiz was confident with the information she already had. Carla was a Rankin, smart and well educated, Colin's sister, single, a survivor, hard worker, confident, a loner and lost. She was exactly what Kiz needed on her team.

Walking back to the hotel, Kiz began to think about the upcoming meeting with the potential investors and principals. Her mind drifted off as she decided to sit for a while on a bench overlooking the Seine across the street from her hotel room. Her thoughts were on the individuals she had invited to the September gathering at the Palace of Fontainebleau.

Fontainebleau was the perfect place. She was pretty sure Eula and Iva would travel over from Melbourne and Germany. Eula had a degree in mathematics and biotech and chemistry from the University of Melbourne. She had taken a part-time role with a research lab in Melbourne and a part-time role with Kline Research, continuing her interests in DNA and predictive modeling. Iva had long since left Landing Enterprise and was working with a select group of colleagues from Sweden, India, Germany, France, and the USA working in human gene transfer and nucleic acid research. She initially studied under Dr. Ken Kline at Kline Research in biomedical research and genetics.

To reconnect face to face after all of these years. Kiz was interested to learn what the women who kidnapped her years ago had to say. The invitation to the women and others was short and direct. Kiz knew the individuals invited would all consider her proposal a gift once they discovered it was part of their destiny to meet.

Kiz invited twelve people to the dinner. Some of the individuals' paths had crossed with hers and were relationships she cherished. The eight of the twelve invitees were from France, Chile, Germany, India, Sweden, Netherlands, Africa and Austria. Each of the eight including Kiz had the desired gene, and the destiny of each of them could only be fulfilled if all of them collaborated and agreed to a common cause. Kiz believed that destiny and cause was world dominance of information.

Kiz's intent was to determine interest and commitment to move forward. Otherwise, she would move forward without all of the power seven and change the world anyway. Did this group have the courage and vision to start something rather remarkable?

The early fall in Paris was beautiful and the night air refreshing. Sitting under a well-lit area and walking path above the River Seine was the perfect place to think and be alone.

Kiz reached into her briefcase, pulled out the draft invitation she'd planned to send to the group of twelve. She wanted to read the invitation out loud to make sure the urgency of the matter was clearly expressed and would cause the invitees to feel a sense of obligation resulting from the content and a need to accept the invitation.

The cream-colored stationery was perfect – clean and crisp, straight forward. Kiz's handwriting was steady and beautifully scripted. Every word had to be perfect, and she couldn't leave anything to misinterpretation. The meeting was urgent, and the expectation was only for the invitees, no proxies.

Kiz read quietly, a light breeze from the river occasionally causing the paper to move slightly. It began:

My future trusted confidant,

Time never stands still. It moves on with or without us. Each day must be our best day … tomorrow is not promised. Today I'm reaching out to you and a select few other dynamic individuals whom I've had the privilege to meet along my life journey. You are receiving this invitation because of something you shared with me. An experience that united us on a shared path toward our destiny is linked in a peculiar way.

I've felt for a while that we need a gathering. There are eight amongst this group who have been identified as carriers of a special "something." I won't say more, but my research and instincts suggest you know who you are I've invited four others outside of the eight to our gathering whose expertise and integrity will be invaluable as members of my team. I'm one of the eight, so each of the seven others will need a similar team. I'll explain more when we convene. I'm sure you'll have better ideas.

The research and information given to me indicate that each member of the group of eight has begun to think about a gathering such as the one I'm suggesting. My intent is to get things moving now and establish a governance structure to allow us to aggressively move forward. The geo-political headwinds are not in our favor, but collectively we can redirect and disrupt current trends.

Comrades, now is our moment to do something important – a game-changing venture, a force that will impact future generations.

A few of you have asked me to stay in touch – and let you know how we can do something important together.

Well, that time has come. I'm asking you to join me on the adventure of our lifetime, an opportunity to influence history and change the world for generations in each of our countries.

Please join me!

With deep respect,

Kiz Lamise Barksdale

What: Game Changer Meeting
Time: 8:00 am–10:00 pm
Where: Palace of Fontainebleau,
Chateau de Fontainebleau
77300 Fontainebleau, France
When: Saturday, September 30, 1980
Host: Kiz Lamise Barksdale
RSVP – SEE RETURNED CARD.

Kiz was pleased with what she read. She placed the draft back in her briefcase and headed toward her hotel, admiring the quaintness and beauty of Paris.

Kiz returned to her room to the sound of the telephone ringing. She reached for the phone and then heard a knock at the door. Distracted, she tried to pull the phone cord line with her as she looked through the peek hole. She could not make out the face.

The knock was harder. Kiz backed away from the door deciding it wasn't smart for her to answer the door.

"Yes, yes?" she said into the phone in a voice loud enough for whoever was at the door to hear.

"Mrs. Barksdale, this is Paul the concierge at the hotel front desk. We have a package for you. Guest Service member Jean will be delivering the package to you shortly. Is that okay?"

As Kiz walked back toward the door, she realized the person had already left.

"I'm sorry I think Jean was already here," Kiz said.

"Oh, I apologize Mrs. Barksdale. Jean saw the package and assumed we had reached out to you. Is it okay for him to return?" Paul continued.

Kiz thought for a brief second. "Let me call you right back." She hung up the phone and then called the front desk to check to make sure everything was safe. The woman who answered the phone did a quick check and let her know it was okay. The person at her door was a hotel employee.

The knock at the door was sounding less urgent and Kiz felt it was okay. But she decided to ask the person to take the package downstairs and she would pick it up later. Kiz was always extra carefully. She thought about Clay and how he insisted she be more careful while traveling.

Kiz smiled at the thought of Clay. He was one of the most trusting people she'd ever known, yet he consistently warned her about being so trusting. Kiz remembered their conversation before she boarded the flight from New York to Paris.

"Do you have everything? What about Erin and Jay's contact information in Paris? Please do call them and let them know you are there. Now Kiz, the Franks would never forgive her if they learned from other sources that you were in Paris for a month and didn't call them," Clay said.

Kiz stood there smiling at that conversation before she left for this trip to Paris. Clay had offered to travel to Paris with her on this particular trip, but he sensed how important it was for her to be alone and have flexibility while she focused on the conference, meeting with Carla and the planning for the investors meeting. She had her hands full as usual.

Kiz reached for the receiver and dialed the concierge.

"Jean speaking, Madame Barksdale, how might I help you this afternoon evening?"

"Good afternoon, Jean, I'm just calling to let you know that everything is okay. I'll pick up the package myself later this evening after dinner," Kiz said.

"That's fine Madame. Would like me to make dinner reservations for you?" Jean asked as he glanced over at the package on his desk addressed to Kiz Lamise Barksdale. The package was marked urgent delivery. A signature was required for pick-up.

"Yes, dinner reservations for just one here at the hotel will be fine for around 6:00 p.m.," Kiz said.

"Okay. I'll take care of it," Jean said. "By the way, Mrs. Barksdale, your package is marked urgent. Are you sure we can't run it up to you now?"

Kiz was hearing some urgency or concern in the young man's voice, so, she decided to walk down to the desk herself and get the package before dinner. After all it was only 3 p.m. and she had plenty of time before dinner.

"Jean, thanks for the offer. I'll be down shortly to pick up the package myself," Kiz said.

"Great. I'll be here at the desk with your package. See you soon," Jean said.

When Kiz picked up the package, she immediately noticed the first attempted delivery was to her New York office and it was then forwarded to her in Paris. The original date was three days ago. As she walked back to the elevator, she recognized the handwriting on the envelope was Jessica, her office assistant's. Jessica had been instructed what to forward and what to hold; plus, she had good instincts.

Kiz sat down at the desk in her room. She opened the package and inside were two envelopes addressed to her with the word "confidential" on the front. She was expecting her assistant to send her the RSVPs. She just did not expect them so soon.

Kiz decided to open the larger envelope first. She was curious about what was inside. She walked over to the desk next to the window that overlooked the city and river, took a piece of cheese and cracker, and then she sat down and picked up the half glass of cabernet she had poured the night before and began to sip wine.

It was a beautiful afternoon. The sun light was boldly reflecting across the river, the free air and mild breeze from the open terrace doors permeated the room. The occasional scent of freshly baked bread reminded her of another wonderful indulgence that made Paris so glorious. A perfect afternoon. She was hopeful the evening would be just as perfect.

She turned her attention again to the envelope. Inside were twelve RSVPs. She'd open each of the responses. Each person had penned a special note to Kiz expressing their desire to listen and learn more about the venture she had in mind. Each of the invitees expressed a desire to know who else was invited, although they did appreciate the need for discretion and confidentiality and would not be disappointment if she decided not to reveal the guest list in advance.

Kiz took another sip of the wine as she looked at the time and determined she would skip the museum and just go to dinner. She had another hour. The second envelop sat there unopened. The day had been perfect. Would the contents of this envelope spoil the day?

Kiz decided to open the envelope, and when she did, she saw embossed at the top of the stationery "From the Desk of Marge Frances Barksdale."

Kiz was shocked and thought to herself, Marge Francis, Clay's aunt and confidante. Why was she writing to her? Kiz had a good relationship with Ms. Marge, but they were not close. Kiz's heart began to beat fast, anticipating some dark secret about Clay was about to be revealed. Then she picked up the bottle of cabernet and poured herself another glass of wine, ate a few pieces of leftover cheese, turned the lamp on, crawled into the lazy chair near the window and fireplace in her hotel room, trying not to get too comfortable. She still had plans for dinner later that evening. She began to read the letter from Clay's Aunt Marge.

Dear Kiz,

I am writing this letter to you in the strictest confidence.
Please do not share the contents with anyone before you
and I meet. You are an amazing woman – I've watched
your life and career for a long time – I admire the work
you are doing and want to help you any way I can. I own
50% of the Landing stock, worth millions. I have more
money than I know what to do with.

Clay shared with me the new venture you are planning
with a very select group of investors. He would be very
upset if he knew I was writing you this letter. I am inter-
ested in your project. I am not asking to join your group
– but I'm willing to be one of your silent angel investors
with an initial gift up to $50 million. We can work out
the terms.

When you are back in New York and have time – call
me. I would love to talk with you face to face and deter-
mine if there is an opportunity for us to work together.
Also, please know that I own substantial real estates in
Manhattan and the upper west side.

Sincerely,

Marge Frances Barksdale

Kiz held the letter in her hands, her mouth was wide open, eyes staring at the letter and millions of thoughts were swirling around in her head. She could smell the scent of vanilla bean and rose, Marge's signature perfume on her hands from the simple yet elegant white linen stationery she held. Kiz took a slow sip of the wine, held the glass mid-way in the air as she stood to look out at the river, the letter dropping from her hands onto the marble tiled floor. She did not attempt to pick it up, but instead took another sip of the wine, moved away from the window and began to think about Clay and his relationship with his aunt. When did Clay tell her and why did she wait until she was in Paris to send the letter?

Kiz knew she had to call Clay. This was beyond an investment opportunity. What were Clay and his Aunt Marge up to? She had to find out.

While Marge Barksdale's letter was intriguing, it would not be enough to dampen the already surging energy and excitement she was feeling after having read earlier the responses from twelve of the most intriguing, smart, and wealthy people she knew in the world. To think that in the next thirty days these individuals would meet with her secretly in Paris. Kiz set the glass down and began to dress for dinner. She was thrilled with the possibility to meet these investors later in the month. And she would not be distracted by the tactics of Landing Enterprise or Shadow Corporation. That included Clay and his family.

The hotel phone in Kiz's room kept ringing. She was in the shower with the room radio on to her favorite Paris jazz station and didn't hear the ring as she sang along with Nina Simone.

Where is she? Clay wondered as her hotel phone kept ringing. He was hoping to talk with her before she left for dinner.

"Sir, there is no answer in Mrs. Barksdale's room. Would you like to leave a message for her or call back?" the hotel operator asked Clay.

"Uhmm... I'll try the call a little later. Thank you," Clay said.

"Sir, I'd be happy to leave a message for Mrs. Barksdale," the operator offered again.

"No, that's okay. I'll try again," Clay said. He knew how independent Kiz was and never wanted her to feel like he was crowding her space. Although Clay really did need to talk with her as soon as possible.

"Okay sir. Have a good evening." Then the operator hung-up the phone

Clay was thinking it was about 5:00 p.m. Paris time. Kiz was probably out walking or visiting with old law school friends. He could never keep up with her. She was always on the run. Kiz loved evening dinners in Paris and would probably have a 7:00 p.m. dinner reservation. There was a chance to catch her at the hotel before dinner.

Clay decided he would wait and call her later; meanwhile, he would set the alarm for mid-night, take a quick hour nap and try calling her. He needed to file a court procedure in the morning, pick-up his ticket for Pairs and stop by his aunt's resident to finalize some papers she wanted him to review. He knew his day and week would be busy- but he had to make the trip to Paris. He knew there was no way he could share the information he had over the telephone, and he also needed to give her a document that might come in handy in case anything ever happened to him or his Aunt Marge. Clay set the alarm and went to sleep.

Kiz turned the shower off and started getting dressed. She checked the time and realized she had plenty of time. It was still early in Paris. She checked the time in New York and thought, Clay was probably napping, drinking or working... his usual routine. He was a night owl. So, anything before mid-night was okay for a coherent conversation.

Ring, ring, ring. The sound of the phone ringing startled Clay. He was in a deep sleep having a crazy dream about tape and fire. He was half awake when he picked up the phone.

"Hello," Clay said.

"Hey sleepy head. What are you doing, napping?" Kiz said in a teasing tone.

Clay hesitated for a moment. "Kiz?"

"Okay, Mr. Barksdale you are busted. Were you expecting someone else?" Kiz said, laughing out loud.

Clay brushed the teasing aside. "How are you doing, sweetheart? I tried to call you about fifteen minutes ago but didn't get an answer. What's up?"

"Ah, I've been here all evening, just got out the shower, getting dressed for dinner. I was just thinking about you and planned to give you a call," Kiz said.

She continued, "I am going to have a quiet dinner alone this evening. What's going on with you?" Kiz asked with a hint of frustration.

Kiz was annoyed with Clay for sharing with his aunt her plans for the Paris dinner and meeting with the investors. Why would he share the plan? What was he up to and would he tell her he told Ms. Marge? How much did he tell her? Kiz was thinking as Clay rambled on about the weather and news stories that were airing. Quickly, she tuned back in as she heard him call her name.

"Kiz, I just received some important information about a woman name Marylee Charles Landrieu – also known as Marylee Dinkins. You need to see this information," Clay said.

He continued, "What if I come over there for the weekend and bring the file with me? You may need my help." He paused then said, "Plus, I miss you so much."

Kiz needed to talk with Clay too about his aunt and the weird letter she received earlier. She was surprised Clay mentioned Marylee Dinkins. It had been a long time since she had heard that name, although she too had done some research on the woman who tried to change her life. And, yes, she missed Clay too. Her decision to spend three months in Paris was something both of them agreed to and knew the reason was important to Kiz.

"Okay, Clay that would be wonderful. Hey, tell me you already made your reservations?" Kiz asked, laughing. She knew Clay.

"I'll be there first thing on Friday morning. Love you!" Clay said, laughing too, as both of them said goodbye.

Kiz gave a heavy sigh, another look at the river before she finished dressing for dinner. She decided to call Carla and follow up on the offer. Perhaps Carla would join her for dinner. Carla could be a tremendous asset to Kiz. Plus, she owed so much to Colin. If only they could have resolved their differences. Perhaps, this was the universe working to give both of them a second chance through Carla, a young lawyer.

Carla Rankin was a tall strikingly beautiful woman. She was a clear blend between her mother and father. She stood at the door of the restaurant talking with the hostess when she saw Kiz enter. Immediately, she walked to give Kiz a warm greeting.

The two women spent the evening chatting about European and US politics. Kiz listened intensely as Carla talked about her life in Paris and desire to move back to the States. After about thirty minutes of small talk, the conversation turned more serious and uncomfortable.

"What happened between you and my sister?" Carla asked.

Kiz anticipated the question, but she wasn't sure how to answer.

"Your sister and I had a complicated childhood," Kiz said.

"I figured it was complicated – but how complicated?" Carla asked.

"Did your sister share anything with you about our child-hood?" Kiz asked.

"Colin would say to me all the time that she loved you more than anyone else in the world and if she had to trade her life to save yours, she would do it," Carla said. "When she was ill, near death really, she told me that something happened when you both were little girls that involved my grandfather, but she wouldn't say much more. In fact, she lost the ability to talk shortly after she started talking about your relationship. She was very sick for about nine months. It was the last few months of her life that she told me about you. She spoke in short phases or words. Things like, "I'm sorry, tell Kiz. Betrayal, Pal, the corpses, Kizzy's mom, gun, rape," Carla said.

Kiz looked at Carla as she spoke. The young woman had no idea of the meaning behind what she just shared. Kiz picked up the glass of water and took a sip, then she began.

"Carla, when Colin and I were young girls – seven years old – we would play near the Susquehanna River. It was my favorite spot in the whole wide world, and I told your sister about it and it became our secret place. One day after school she decided to follow me to the river as she would do often. Dorothy, your oldest sister saw Colin and me leave school and walking the wrong way, toward the colored part of town. Dorothy decided to follow us to see what was going on.

"When Colin and I got to the river we saw three boys there sitting on the bank of the river, three white boys. That was unusual because of the part of town it was. There was usually no one on the edge. We walked on by the boys. No one said a word. We were probably five minutes into our walk before we heard a scream. It was Dorothy. The three boys had dragged her to the ground and were trying to rape her. Two of the boys were holding her down and the other one was on top of her. We saw my two brothers come from a different direction… my older brothers were in the same grade as Dorothy, so they knew each other. They had followed her, wondering where she was going by herself. Colin and I witnessed my brothers and the three white boys fighting. One of the boys pushed Dorothy against a tree. She fell and hit her head. The boys all got scared and ran away in different directions.

"Dorothy was okay. But she later lied about what happened, and Colin, who saw the entire thing, never spoke up or told the truth about what actually happened. My brothers saw us as they ran away. Dorothy said that two black boys dragged her to the river from school and tried to rape her and that three white boys who she did not know tried to save her. She said the boys all ran after a fight started and she did not know any of them. She never mentioned that she was following Colin and me that day. Dorothy committed suicide a few years later. She was a freshman in college. Her body was found in the Hudson River. A note was found in her dorm room and it read, 'I lied and I'm sorry,'" Kiz said.

"Colin never told me why Dorothy killed herself… she just said there was an accident years earlier. Dorothy hit her head and was never the same afterwards," Carla said.

"Well, Colin and I talked about her accident when we met in New York; it was one of several things we discussed. I can't blame Dorothy for what she did, but she did cause a lot of pain for a lot of people when she should have told the truth," Kiz said.

"My two brothers were rumored to be the villains, and that incident hung over their heads for years. It was only when the suicide note was found that my brothers got their lives back. I tried to tell my parents what actually happened, but they told me to shut up and not talk about it again. My brothers were unusually quiet too.

"I remembered my brother Leon saying to me, 'Kizzy, you are too young to understand what's going on, and you'll never understand what it's like to be a black boy. You are too young to understand. Plus you are a girl. Bad things happen to good people. Stay out of it. Plus, no one will ever believe our story over the white boys' stories and Dorothy and Collin will never tell the truth. Larry and I will be okay.'

"My father was livid, and my mom was scared," Kiz continued.

"Ms. Kiz, was this related to your mother's death and the corpses?" Carla asked.

"What do you know about the corpses?" Kiz asked, somewhat surprised by Carla's directness.

Chapter 15

Clay

How would he even begin to share with Kiz what he had learned about Marylee and Richard Dinkins and the role the Dinkins' played in her mother's death? Clay moved the file off the coffee table and into his briefcase. He wanted to check on a possible connection between Marylee and her old friend at Shadow Corporation.

It was around 7:30 a.m., Wednesday morning. NBC News was on in the background. Coffee was brewing in the kitchen, and Clay had just finished shaving. He had an early-morning court appointment and needed to stop by his office for a brief meeting. He had an appointment with his Aunt Marge at noon. He promised his parents he would stop in to see them before the week was over. Now that his trip to Paris was confirmed for Friday, he would try to see his parents this evening. He thought he'd better give his mom and dad a call to see if tonight would be good for them.

Clay finished dressing, went into his study to call his parents. He heard a tapping sound – but thought nothing of it and continued to dial his parents' number.

"Hello," his father answered the phone.

"Good morning, Dad," Clay said, distracted by an unusual sound in the other room. "Dad, I was wondering if you and mom were free for dinner tonight. Hold on dad, I need to check something – sounds like someone is at the door." Clay placed the receiver on the desk, his father patiently waiting on the other end.

"Coming, coming," Clay repeated. The buzzing of the doorbell caught him off guard. He wasn't expecting anyone, and the doorman would usually call up first, before allowing guests. Only residents had the ability to enter and leave without being escorted. Strange, Clay thought as he reached to open the door without thinking much more about how the unusual occurrence really was. Maybe it's a resident needing a favor.

Everything became a blur quickly.

Holy shit – is this how it's supposed to end, Clay thought as he felt his body being lifted in mid-air and something perhaps plastic being placed over his head. He could feel the strong grip of hands carrying his body. It felt like he was being carried in midair. He couldn't move his head, he gasped for air. There was none. There were no tears but a trace of sadness. In the flash of the moment, he thought about Kiz. *What would they tell her about how he died? What am I hearing?* He could faintly hear the men talking. His body suddenly hitting something hard, he could not breathe. He thought of the lessons he learned from his swimming days and the games they would play as kids. Could he count to a thousand and hold this breath? He thought he'd give it a try. The sounds of something tearing and then a tightening against his body distracted him. He'd try again to count.

"Get the tape, Joe. Let's finish wrapping him up."

"Got it," another voice said. "You get the head and work down, and I'll start with the feet. But leave the plastic over his head. We can't take any chances, or the boss will not pay us if any evidence is left behind," the strange voice said.

Clay's father remained on the line. He could hear movement on the other end and men talking but he could not distinguish what they were saying. He thought it a bit odd that Clay didn't pick up the phone to end the conversation, a simple yes or no about dinner wouldn't take long no matter how busy he was. Perhaps he had forgotten his father was on the other end. Then he clearly heard something strange.

"Mark did you bring the gasoline?" the voice asked.

"Yes, but do you think we need to use it? Plan B might be more efficient," the second voice stated.

Clay's father was alarmed with what he heard. He immediately hung up the phone and tried to dial the police.

Mark, one of the men in the room heard the buzzing sound of a phone off the hook. He looked around and noticed the receiver on the desk, suggesting that Clay was talking with someone before they arrived. Whoever was on the phone had just hung up.

Once the men had taped up Clay, they began to look for the files they were instructed to find. They needed to hurry, because whoever was on that phone might be calling the police or the building security. They would abandon their plans for disposing of the body and gather the files and leave. Time was of the essence.

"There it is," said one of the men. There on the kitchen counter was a file marked confidential and a second file marked important documents sitting next to a half-filled coffee cup.

"Go ahead, we need to check these," said the taller of the two men. The men opened each of the files to check for a certain marking to help them identify the files they were looking for.

"What? … Something's wrong," the shorter of the men blurted out in alarm. To their surprise, neither of the files had the markings.

"Paul, I'm sure these are the files we're instructed to bring back," the taller of the men said.

Both men gathered the manila folders. They quickly left the residence the same way they entered. The entire episode took less than twenty minutes.

Clay could barely see the images in front of him through the plastic bag as his breathing became more difficult. His eyes began to widen as fear overtook his emotions. He felt like he was being picked up and carried again. He couldn't breathe – he was losing it. He tried to smile and out of the blurriness of the plastic there she sat, the little seven-year-old girl he rescued over 30 years ago. He tried to open his eyes… not sure if he was dead or not. Darkness was all around him – then a light from somewhere far away was shining in his direction. Clay tried to move – but he couldn't. He thought

– I must be dead. He heard a familiar voice as he faded in and out of consciousness – seeing images of people with whom he had unfinished business.

'Grandpa is that you?' Clay mimicked with his lips. He could not speak, his energy was gone. He thought he heard his grandfather say, "Yes, my son, I am with you. Be strong, they are coming for you." Then the voice ended, and the image disappeared.

Winston Barksdale, Clay's grandfather, died five years earlier; he left twenty-five percent of his entire estate, including his shares in Landing Enterprise, to his grandchildren, and the other seventy-five percent was spilt between his two children, Clay's father and his Aunt Marge. Both Clay's father and aunt had already inherited millions from their grandfather (Clay's great-grandfather). The family's wealth was astonishing.

Clay Barksdale lay still, having lost consciousness. In a sea of memories, an inner peace complicated with a few regrets. His wealth never entering his mind, he knew the reason for this dreadful ending. Hopefully, Kiz would never know that he betrayed her, too.

"Mr. Barksdale, please stay with us," the paramedics repeated as they placed the oxygen mask over Clay's face. "Please."

Clay's face felt heavy. There was something on his nose and he couldn't breathe freely. Something was happening. He couldn't determine what before he drifted back to when he and Mason first met Kizzy.

"Do you think he's going to make it?" the policeman asked.

"There is a ninety-eight percent chance he won't make it," the paramedic said.

"Somebody really wanted him dead! When we see these types of crimes they are usually connected with the underworld," the police detective said.

The police detectives had given the okay to unwrap the tape from his body. The way his body was wrapped reminded the detective of an old unsolved case he read about from the 50s when he was at the police academy. Maybe the gasoline and the way the body was wrapped made him think of that case from down in Harrisburg.

Clay was not yet pronounced dead. The scene was clearly a crime scene but had not yet been called a murder scene. Clay's body was removed from the scene and placed in a waiting ambulance and taken to Mount Sinai Hospital.

"How long has he been unconscious?" Dr. Ward, the emergency doctor asked the paramedics as they rolled Clay into the emergency room.

"We found him pretty much unresponsive when we got to him about twelve minutes ago," responded one of the EMTs.

"Okay. We'll take it from here," Dr. Ward said.

The doorman stood in the hall with the police as the Medical Emergency team took Clay from his condo… the condo was basically in order- there were minimum signs that anything was out of order or taken. Either robbery was not the motive, and the capture or death of the male occupant was the primary reason for the invasion. A can of gasoline was sitting on the floor near where Clay's body had been removed.

A stripe of tape was found next to the phone in Clay's office and a black smudge was on the kitchen counter. The police took pictures and tested the condo for fingerprints. If the father's call, the doorman and security calls and timelines all matched up, then whoever entered the residence had less than 15 minutes to do whatever they came to do and escape without being spotted a second time.

The condo security camera caught two men entering the condo from the delivery entrance. Somehow, they had secured a special key to the building and had gone almost unnoticed. The only other resident on the floor that Kiz and Clay occupied alerted the doorman of strange noises and the smell of gasoline on the floor coming from the Barksdale residence. The concierge tried calling Clay's condo, but the phone was disconnected. At the same time, the doorman alerted security and they saw the men on Clay's floor. The security officer tried to take the elevator up to Clay's floor, but the elevator was stuck in the top floor. So, the security officer called the police for back-up before taking the emergency elevator himself.

Kiz was returning from dinner with colleagues – in a pretty good mood. The conference was one of her favorites and she was excited to meet with Carla tomorrow evening and spend the weekend with Clay in Paris. She was curious about the information he wanted to share with her.

"Good evening Mrs. Barksdale, may I help you?" the front desk clerk greeted her as she walked up to the reception desk.

"Good evening," Kiz said. "I am checking for messages. I'm in room 222."

"Madame, you have three messages," the front desk clerk said as he handed Kiz the messages.

Kiz quickly looked at the messages. The first was from Mount Sini Hospital, New York: "Please call Dr. Ward ASAP." The second was from the New York City Police Department: "Please call Detective Foster." And the third message was from Marge Frances Barksdale. She froze.

Clay Barksdale was pronounced dead at 3:30 p.m. ET. His death was ruled homicide. The details and news were overwhelming. Being a lawyer, Kiz knew the right questions to ask and keep her composure as she learned details from Dr. Ward.

Marge was a basket case, and Kiz tried to calm her. Other Barksdales were at the family home with Marge. Dr. Ward tried to reassure Kiz that Clay did not suffer at the end. Kiz knew better – after she read the police report.

"Hello Carmen. This is Kiz. How are you doing?"

"Kiz, where are you and how are you doing? We just got the news about Clay – it's all over the TV… Dad and everybody are worried. No one has been able to reach you. Where are you, and are you okay?" Carmen asked.

"Yes, yes, I'm fine," Kiz said. "I'm in Paris. Just got the news myself about an hour ago. I'm okay. I'll be back in New York tomorrow night. The soonest I could get a flight back to the States."

"Kiz, is there anything I can do to help you? I'm available to come up to New York and help you with the funeral arrangements and anything else you need," Carmen asked.

"Carmen, thank you. All of this happened so fast. But yes. Let me call you after I get to New York. My understanding is the condo is considered a crime scene, so I might not want to stay there. I will let you know where I'm staying and we can take it from there," Kiz said.

"Okay Kiz. We all love you so much and Clay too, this is just not fair," Carmen said as Kiz interrupted her.

"Okay Carmen, I gotta go. Give my love to everyone and I'll be in touch once I'm back in the States. Talk soon," Kiz said as she hung up.

Kiz's guest appearance at the conference was scheduled for first thing in morning. She decided to keep her appearance and the extra time would give her time to clear her head before facing the cameras back home and all the questions about Clay's death. Kiz was thinking like a lawyer, not as a grieving wife. She knew that would come.

She would follow up on dinner with Carla tomorrow night and leave for the airport the next morning to catch her flight to New York. The phone was ringing.

"Hello," Kiz answered.

"Mrs. Barksdale, this is Pierre the hotel manager. We are calling to see if everything is okay."

Kiz paused, trying to decide how much to reveal. Then she responded, "Thanks for calling Pierre. I do have an emergency back home and will need to check-out early. But I do plan to return for my extended stay. My best guess is I'll be back in the States for a couple weeks, returning later in the month. I will know more tomorrow afternoon."

"We are here to support you in any way we can Mrs. Barksdale. Please let us know whatever you need," Pierre said.

"I will," Kiz said. Then they both hung-up.

Kiz's Trip Back to the USA for Clay's Funeral

The trip back to the States seemed longer than usual, although Kiz had so much to think about. She had a funeral to arrange, planning the dinner with the twelve guests and handling Clay's estate. She already was finding it difficult to imagine what her life would be like without Clay – he was her everything. She had loved him all of her life in so many different ways. She often wondered what life would be like when he was gone. Now she would experience that. Her thoughts were interrupted by the passenger sitting next to her.

"Excuse me, Ms., I just want to get up and use the rest room." The passenger was an older man in his sixties.

"Of course," Kiz said as she stood up. She glanced over to the passenger's seat and saw he was reading a book. She sat back down and wondered who the stranger was sitting next to her, although she was not in any mood to talk.

"Thank you," the passenger said again as he returned.

Kiz stood up to let the man pass.

"My name is Gene Conrad. I'm from Philadelphia," the man said.

Kiz introduced herself. "Hello, my name is Kiz Barksdale."

Gene Conrad continued, "I noticed you were wiping tears from your eyes for the last thirty minutes of this flight. Would it be helpful to talk with a stranger about what's bothering you?"

Kiz looked over again. "What are you reading?" she asked.

He smiled at her and said, "These are my daily teachings and affirmations. Mostly a collection of Hemingway and Gandhi. He reached over to hand Kiz a small book opened to a familiar passage.

Chapter 16

The Perch – The Beginning

T he guests started to arrive at the hotel, each anxious to see who else would be there.

Kiz's invitation was as mysterious as Kiz. She had arranged for each of them to stay at different hotels throughout Paris. She was sensitive to their cultures and personal preferences.

Kiz did not want the guests to meet each other prior to the gathering, which was the reason for separating them during their stay in Paris. A few of the guests had a second residence in Paris, thus declining the need for hotel accommodations; another had a family hotel in Paris and preferred that option. The other women stayed at the hotel recommended for them by Kiz.

Saturday, January 30, 1996, the day of the meeting would be an important date.

Kiz, watched as the group began to enter the meeting room. Most of the guests had never met each other. They would take the assigned seats given to them at the door.

Arrangements were made for each of the guests to arrive at different times.

When the guests arrived, they were greeted at the door by Carla Rankin, who handed each of them an envelope with their names handwritten on the cover and a table note regarding the seating arrangements.

Inside were further confidential instructions and a personalized, detailed profile about each person's destiny. The guests were only given information about themselves along with an invitation to a follow-up meeting in New York City. The seven already knew who they were. They just had never been together in one setting. They represented the major continents of the world.

The other five guests were invited to join the power seven for this initial meeting. No documents were allowed to leave the room. The guests were instructed to read the materials in silence. Food was served at different times throughout the day while the guest read and reflected. No notes or recordings were allowed. After all the materials were read and the dinner completed, Kiz came out to greet each of the guests individually in the space that had been set aside for them. She thanked each of them for coming and gave a powerful speech about destiny to close the long day. Throughout the day Kiz would meet with each of the guests to discuss the profiles, the destiny project and answer any questions. She had each guest exit to separate rooms for the in-depth conversations.

There was no socializing between the guests because of the sensitivity of the information. The guests all understood and welcomed the opportunity to meet as a smaller group in New York to move the destiny project forward.

The day and evening spent at Palace Fontainebleau was a huge success – Kiz's plan was moving forward.

The next morning

Kiz stood on the balcony overlooking the River Seine. She would leave Paris in a few days and head back to the United States. She had unfinished business there and felt she needed to help some old friends navigate through the dangerous path ahead. She picked up the New York Times that had been delivered to her room; although the paper was a day behind, she still felt a need to keep up with what was happening back home.

The mysterious death of Marylee Charles Landrieu was the headline of the paper. The small piece read: New York City. An older woman known in certain circle for clandestine activities and unusual access was found dead in Midtown this morning by a jogger.

The article raised a red flag for Kiz. What was it Clay had wanted to show her, and was it in any way connected to the black magic underground culture in New Orleans?

The article went on to say that the woman's body was bound and burned; her corpse was found by a jogger this morning sitting upright on a bench in Central Park. It appeared she was burned alive.

Kiz could not help but think about her own experience some so many years ago at school when the dead corpses were found. Marylee was at the center of that disastrous day, the day she witnessed the corpse, her mother's murder and the kidnapping.

Who was Marylee Charles Landrieu? "Who was she, really?" Kiz wondered aloud. "Who was Marylee Charles Landrieu? Rev. Dinkins' wife."

Marylee was the illegitimate daughter of Barry Charles Lewis, Sr., the founder of Shadow Corporation; her half-brother was Barry Charles Lewis, Jr., an heir to Shadow Corporation and the current president. Marylee's mother and Barry Martin (her half-brother) were united in a blizzard sacrifice set-up by Marylee's grandmother, Genevieve, a practicing witch who lived in New Orleans. Marylee's mother was conceived via an alliance between her grandmother and Martin Lewis who was a slave owner. Marylee was cursed as a fetus in her mother's womb. Some called it a bad seed, since her mother went insane during her birth and killed herself. The father of the child was always thought to be one of the Lewis's sons. Marylee grew up in a private boarding school totally funded by the Lewis family and far away from her aging grandmother. She never saw or knew any of her mother's family – the Lewis family made sure of that. Marylee spent her entire life working in some capacity or with some connection to the Lewis family and Shadow Corporation.

Marylee was smart; so much so that old man Lewis felt that if she had been a man, she would have been his pick over his sons to run Shadow Corporation. But she was a girl and a colored girl at that (but she had his blood there was no denying that fact; she looked like a Lewis). Fair skin, tall and skinny, curly dark brown hair and eyes and the nose that described most of the women in the Lewis family so, he did the only thing he knew how to do – keep his distance, make sure she got a good education, keep the family secrets from her and make sure she always had a job.

Marylee was a stubborn kid. She had plans of her own. She was not interested in college, so she took on her first full-time job at Shadow Corporation in New York in the investigative unit, or, as nicknamed by colleagues, the "crime" or "undercover" unit.

Kiz was riveted by what she was reading. Clay had sent her a copy of the report he kept in a private safe they had in an extra apartment in lower Manhattan, the apartment she first rented after graduating from law school. They thought it had a certain sentimental value, so they bought the building and redid the apartment and called it their other New York residence. Mostly it was Kiz's escape from the glitz of the upper west side. The people who killed Clay must have been looking for this letter, Kiz thought, or was there something else. She would look more thoroughly through the apartment for additional information. The police had a few clues; they had identified the men from the security camera – but so far neither man was talking. The police were frustrated. But the case was still young. Clay's aunt was livid with the progress and talked to the police chief every day. The Barksdale family influence in New York was significant and Landing Enterprise was a premier company; to have an heir to the company murdered brought major attention throughout the world.

He watched her from inside the hotel suite as she slowly closed the door to the balcony. She placed the paper on the desk. She stared at him.

"Well, I think you are finally free, Kiz. You took care of them both – and you have the perfect alibi," he said.

"Mason – Clay was your best friend. Why … no! How could you dismiss him in such a crude way?" Kiz asked.

"Oh Kiz, I've told you a thousand times what Clay's motives were. Yes, I'll admit he did love you in a weird way… but his obsession with taking over Landing from his father and uncles outweighed his love for you," Mason said.

"So, where do we go from here?" Kiz asked as she poured herself a glass of wine, while acknowledging the glass Mason had already poured for himself.

"I've been giving this a lot of thought, Kiz. And first you and I need to sort out what's next for us," Mason stated as he stood and moved closer to Kiz.

"Mason, not now. We are going to have to be very careful over the next several months or year… we can't afford anyone suspecting that there's more between us then just close friendship," Kiz said.

"You are right," Mason said as he backed off. In his heart, he knew that Kiz would find a way to get rid of him too. She was incapable of loving anyone – except an imaginary friend who stayed with her from her childhood – The Watcher. Mason and Clay had discussed while dinking together over the many years of the friendship whether she knew this imaginary friend was real or not. Kiz had an extraordinary imagination, and her appetite for danger and lust for life made it difficult for any one person to fulfill her needs. Clay knew that about her and always suspected she was involved with someone else. But he never expressed to Mason that he suspected him. Mason watched Kiz, wondering how she would get rid of him.

Kiz walked over to Mason. The two stood facing each other without a word. Their eyes were full of memories, special moments, hopes, desires, and passion. No words were spoken, no words were needed. Then their hands touched. They embraced tightly, holding each other so tightly, desire mounting in both of their bodies – reminding them of the deep satisfaction they shared when their bodies connected. But the feeling was interrupted by the realization that this was the end. Mason pulled away first. He took a step back, held Kiz's shoulders and looked at her one more time.

"Goodbye, my love. I hope we meet again in our next life. Maybe then – things will be different," Mason said. He walked out of the hotel door.

"Mason," Kiz cried out. "Mason!"

The door shut.... The room was quiet. Kiz stood in silence. Mason stood on the other side of the door and whispered, "I will always love you." Waiting for him was his destiny. He walked down the hall with the two men who were waiting for him.

Chapter 17

The End

"Ladies and Gentlemen, this ending could just as easily be the beginning. I've shared with you the transition, how we got to this day," Kiz said.

"My story is just one of many to be told. Today, I'm proud to introduce you to six amazing women who have helped make this day and beginning possible," Kiz continued.

"Each of these women has amazing stories to tell. You heard my story this evening. But, over time you'll hear from each of them about their journey to this day."

"Aayan, Nayana, Sara, Scarlett, Abigail and Melinda are the women who will help shape the world. Together, we represent the world, Africa, Asia, Australia/Oceania, Europe, North and South America. The team they have assembled is diverse, smart, talented, enterprising, and committed to this future we want to help define and the past to leave behind," Kiz continued.

Today, I'm proud to announce the launch of Growth Resources Corporation, a woman-led enterprise with business operations on seven continents. Our focused is the next generation of technology connectivity and collaborative platforms across thousands of distribution channels and industries. We are a private enterprise seeking to do good in the world. Today, our valuation is set at $200 trillion dollars, and our goal is to triple that within the next eight years to over a $600 trillion dollars," Kiz said.

"We, the seven of us, have invested our time, money, and talents to make this day possible. Perhaps the most import thing we've done was to acquire two pioneering companies in the area of predictive modeling and leveraged their capabilities and research to move this company forward to the next generation of leadership and competitiveness in the global market. Let me now introduce the women who will change the world of commerce."

Aayan (Africa)
Nayanna (Asia/India)
Sara (Asia/India)
Scarlett (Australia/Oceania)
Abigail (Europe)
Melinda (South America)
Kiz (North America)

The voice

"'Little girl little girl who are you. Tell me your name," the strange voice in her head would ask her over and over again.

"'I am me… I am Kizzy,' she would reply."

Kizzy sat there with her hands cupped under her chin helping to hold her head up. Her eyes were bright, and in the fullness of the sun and the clarity of which she saw the world was beyond anyone's imagination. She smiled but faintly. She knew even as a child she had so much to do.

Kiz had not heard the voice since she was a child. Then today, the voice returned. The voice: "I knew you a long time ago. I had to let you go to become me."

"Who are you and what do you want? Why are you back?" Kiz asked out of curiosity.

The voice was silent for a few seconds. Then Kiz heard.

"I am you and you are now me. We are one."

The beginning, 2022: Kiz, age seventy

She stood behind the stage of the large auditorium. Her purple dress, gold necklace, silver short grey hair, and black shoes matched perfectly with the stage's dark blue draped curtain backdrop and the light grey heavily cushioned chair that was set up for her on a raised platform.

The staging was perfect.

As Kiz continued to peek out from behind the curtain, she could see the crowd gathering inside the newly remodeled neo-classical auditorium. They were there to meet and hear the retiring Supreme Court Justice share her extraordinarily complex, successful and controversial life story. The room filled up quickly – the event had sold out almost immediately; over 2,500 people were expected to be there.

Kiz held on tightly to the arm of the black wrought iron chair next to her. The auditorium was quiet as Dr. Edward Anderson Johnson, an old colleague from the university where the two had taught law, approached the podium to introduce Kiz.

While Dr. Johnson was introducing Kiz, she surveyed the audience from behind the stage. The lights were blinding from the angle where she stood. She blinked her eyes hoping to see more clearly, and the faces were still a blur, but they were becoming clearer. She saw some familiar faces – old and new friends, former colleagues, strangers, and lots of young people.

Kiz surveyed the crowd for a particular person. She dropped her head in slight disappointment when there was no sign of him. The applause continued as she moved from behind the curtain to the stage.

Dr. Johnson continued, "Again, Ladies and Gentlemen, let's give a warm welcome to our special storyteller, exemplar businesswoman and humanitarian, the honorable Judge Kiz Lamise Barksdale." The thunderous applause erupted again. Kiz walked across the stage.

Kiz was a storyteller, and she enjoyed communicating with her audience using a conversational style. A dark grey, cushioned, high-back chair was placed at the center of the stage on plush navy carpet that covered a large, elevated riser. The riser was to help with audience viewing and gave Kiz a specially designed perch from which to tell her story.

Folded on the arm of the chair was a black silk and wool shawl. A small coffee table was angled to the right of the chair where, arranged neatly, there were a glass of water, a pair of glasses, a notebook and pen.

Behind the chair on both sides were tall brass ornate floor lamps both with beige round beveled shades.

The applause continued for several minutes. Kiz's life and career had been extraordinary.

Kiz thought again about how beautiful the remodeled auditorium was, the deep blue stage backdrop, the grey-colored chairs and the paneled walls with the beautiful artwork. The lighting and ceiling resembled the many cathedrals she had visited in Europe. The choice to wear the purple dress this evening was a good one.

Kiz Lamise Barksdale at seventy years old was ready for the first time to share her life story and perhaps the truth. In the empty space between the applause and her opening words, she felt the tingle of a familiar caress as his hands laid firmly on her shoulders. She closed her eyes with a sense of knowing while his hands moved smoothly down her arms. She felt the light touch of his moist lips on the right side of her neck. She opened her eyes as the applause ended. He had filled the empty space of time.

Kiz stood to acknowledge and thank the audience for their generous welcome, and she then summoned her inner child to join her on stage. Kizzy smiled. I had arrived.

I'm the Watcher, the narrator of this story.

Printed in the USA
CPSIA information can be obtained
at www.ICGtesting.com
LVHW011314041024
792844LV00005B/876

9 781662 893131